Candlefor

Flora Jane Thompson was born in 1876 at Juniper Hill, a hamlet on the borders of Oxfordshire and Northamptonshire. After leaving school, h̶ was sent as assistant to the postm̶ town eight miles away, and was letters in a locked leather bag to t connection with the Post Office. later became a postmaster. His wo she obtained from the public libr translation, as well as Ibsen and th

especially Shaw and Yeats. Her first book was a collection of poems, *Bog Myrtle and Peat*. However, she is best remembered for three auto-biographical volumes: *Lark Rise* (1939), *Over to Candleford* (1941) and *Candleford Green* (1943), reissued in one volume as *Lark Rise to Candleford* (1945). A fourth volume, *Still Glides the Stream*, was published posthu-mously in 1948. Flora Thompson died at Brixham, Devon, on 21 May 1947.

FLORA THOMPSON

Candleford Green

PENGUIN BOOKS

PENGUIN CLASSICS

Published by the Penguin Group
Penguin Books Ltd, 80 Strand, London wc2r 0rl, England
Penguin Group (USA) Inc., 375 Hudson Street, New York, New York 10014, USA
Penguin Group (Canada), 90 Eglinton Avenue East, Suite 700, Toronto, Ontario, Canada m4p 2y3
(a division of Pearson Penguin Canada Inc.)
Penguin Ireland, 25 St Stephen's Green, Dublin 2, Ireland
(a division of Penguin Books Ltd)
Penguin Group (Australia), 250 Camberwell Road, Camberwell, Victoria 3124, Australia
(a division of Pearson Australia Group Pty Ltd)
Penguin Books India Pvt Ltd, 11 Community Centre, Panchsheel Park, New Delhi – 110 017, India
Penguin Group (NZ), 67 Apollo Drive, Rosedale, North Shore 0632, New Zealand
(a division of Pearson New Zealand Ltd)
Penguin Books (South Africa) (Pty) Ltd, 24 Sturdee Avenue, Rosebank, Johannesburg 2196, South Africa

Penguin Books Ltd, Registered Offices: 80 Strand, London wc2r 0rl, England

www.penguin.com

First published by Oxford University Press 1943
Published in Penguin Classics 2009
This film and TV tie-in edition published 2009
By arrangement with the BBC
BBC © BBC 1996
The BBC logo is a registered trademark of the
British Broadcasting Corporation and is used under license.

1

Set in 10.5/13 pt PostScript Monotype Dante
Typeset by Rowland Phototypesetting Ltd, Bury St Edmunds, Suffolk
Printed in England by Clays Ltd, St Ives plc

978-0-141-19013-6

www.greenpenguin.co.uk

Mixed Sources
Product group from well-managed
forests and other controlled sources
www.fsc.org Cert no. SA-COC-1592
© 1996 Forest Stewardship Council

Penguin Books is committed to a sustainable future
for our business, our readers and our planet.
The book in your hands is made from paper
certified by the Forest Stewardship Council.

Contents

I

From One Small World to Another

Laura sat up beside her father on the high front seat of the spring-cart and waved to the neighbours. 'Good-bye, Laura! Good-bye!' they called. 'Mind you be a good gal, now!' and Laura, as she turned to smile and wave back to them, tried not to look too conscious of her new frock and hat and the brand-new trunk (with her initials) roped on to the back seat.

As the cart moved on, more women came to their doors to see what the sound of wheels meant at that time in the morning. It was not the coalman's or the fish-hawker's day, the baker was not due for hours, and the appearance of any other wheeled vehicle than theirs always caused a mild sensation in that secluded hamlet. When they saw Laura and her new trunk, the women remained on their doorsteps to wave their farewells, then, before the cart had turned into the road from the rutted lane, little groups began forming.

Her going seemed to be causing quite a stir in the hamlet. Not because the sight of a young girl going out in the world to earn her own living was an uncommon one there – all the hamlet girls left home for that purpose, some of them at a much earlier age than Laura – but they usually went on foot, carrying bundles, or their fathers pushed their boxes on wheelbarrows to the railway station in the nearest town the night before, while, for Laura's departure, the innkeeper's pony and cart had been hired.

That, of course, was because Candleford Green, although only eight miles distant, was on another line of railway than that which ran through the market town, and to have gone there by train would have meant two changes and a long wait at the Junction; but the spring-cart brought a spice of novelty into her departure which made 'something to talk about', as the saying went there. At the beginning of the eighteen-nineties any new subject for conversation was precious in such places.

Laura was fourteen and a half, and the thick pigtail of hair which had so far hung down her back had that morning been looped up once and tied with a big black ribbon bow on her neck. When they had first known that she was to go to work in the Post Office at Candleford Green her mother had wondered if she ought not to wear her hair done up with hairpins, grown-up fashion, but when she saw a girl behind the Post Office counter at Sherston wearing hers in a loop with a bow she had felt sure that that was the proper way for Laura to do hers. So the ribbon was bought – black, of course, for her mother said the bright-coloured ribbons most country girls wore made them look like horses, all plaited and beribboned for a fair. 'And mind you sponge and press it often,' she had said, 'for it cost good money. And when you come to buy your own clothes, always buy the best you can afford. It pays in the end.' But Laura could not bear to think of her mother just then; the parting was too recent.

So she thought of her new trunk. This contained – as well as her everyday clothes and her personal treasures, including her collection of pressed flowers, a lock of her baby brother's fair hair, and a penny exercise book, presented by her brother Edmund and inscribed by him *Laura's Journal*, in which she had promised to write every night – what her mother had spoken of as 'three of everything', all made of stout white calico and trimmed with crochet edging.

'No child of mine,' her mother had often declared, 'shall go out in the world without a good outfit. I'd rather starve!' and when the time had come to get Laura ready for Candleford Green the calico, bought secretly from time to time in lengths, had been brought out from its hiding-place to be made up and trimmed with the edging she had been making for months. 'I told you it would come in handy for something at some time,' she had said, but Laura knew by her arch little smile she had meant it for her all along.

Her father had made and polished the trunk and studded it with her initials in bright, brass-headed nails, and, deep down in one corner of it, wrapped in tissue paper, was the new half-crown he had given her.

The contents of the trunk, the clothes she was wearing, youth and health, and a meagre education, plus a curious assortment of scraps of knowledge she had picked up in the course of her reading, were her only assets. In fitting her out, her parents had done all they could for her. They had four younger children now to be provided for. Her future must depend upon herself and what opportunities might offer. But she had no idea of the slenderness of her equipment for life and no fears for the distant future which stretched before her, years and years in which anything might happen. She could not imagine herself married, or old, and it did not seem possible that she would ever die.

Any qualms she felt were for the immediate future, when she, who had so far only known her cottage home and the homes of a few relatives, would be living in some one else's house, where she would work and be paid for her work and where the work she was to do had still to be learnt. She was much afraid she would not know what she ought to do, or where to find things, or would make mistakes and be thought stupid.

The postmistress of Candleford Green, it was true, was no stranger, but an old girlhood's friend of her mother. Laura had been to her house several times and had liked her, and she thought Miss Lane had liked her. But that only seemed to make the new relationship more difficult. Should she treat Miss Lane as an old friend of the family, or strictly as a new employer? Her mother, when appealed to, had laughed and said: 'God bless the child! always looking for trouble! What is there to worry about? Just be your own natural self and Dorcas I'm sure'll be hers. Though, when it comes to that, perhaps you'd better not go on Cousin Dorcasing her. That was all right when you were a visitor, but now it'd better be "Miss Lane".'

As they lurched out of the rutted road which led round the hamlet, her father urged on the pony. He was not a patient man and there had been too many farewells to suit his taste. 'What a lot!' he muttered. 'You can't so much as hire a horse and cart for a day without creating a nine days' wonder in this place!' But Laura thought it was kind of the neighbours to wish her well. 'Go and get rich and fat,' kind old Mrs Braby had advised; 'and whatever y'do, don't 'ee forget them at home.' Rich she could never be, her starting salary of half a crown a week would leave no margin for saving, and getting fat seemed more improbable still to tall, lanky fourteen – 'like a molern, all legs and wings', as the neighbours had often called her – but she would never forget those at home: that she could promise.

She turned and looked back over green cornfields at the huddle of grey cottages, one of which was her home, and pictured her mother ironing and her little sisters playing round the doorway, and wondered if her favourite brother would miss her when he came home from school and if he would remember to water her garden and give her white rabbit, Florizel, plenty of green leaves, and if he would care to read her new journal when she sent it to him, or would think it silly, as he sometimes did her writing.

But it was May and the warm wind dried her eyes and soothed her sore eyelids, and the roadside banks were covered with the tiny spring flowers she loved, stitchwort and celandine and whole sheets of speedwell, which Laura knew as angel's eyes, and somewhere in the budding green hedgerow a blackbird was singing. Who could be sad on such a day! At one place she saw cowslips in a meadow and asked her father to wait while she gathered a bunch to take as an offering to Miss Lane. Back in her seat, she buried her face in the big fragrant bunch and, ever after, the scent of cowslips reminded her of that morning in May.

When, about midday, they passed through a village, she held the reins while her father went into the inn for a pint of ale for himself and brought out for her a tall tumbler of sweet, fizzing orangeade. She sat in state on her high seat and sipped it gently in the grown-up way she had seen farmers' wives in gigs sipping their drinks before the inn at home, and it pleased her to imagine that the elderly clergyman who glanced her way in passing was wondering who that interesting-looking girl in the spring-cart could be, although she knew very well in sober fact he was more probably thinking about his next Sunday's sermon, or trying to decide whether or not he owed a parochial call at the next house he had to pass. At fourteen it is intolerable to resign every claim to distinction. Her hair was soft and thick and brown and she had rather nice brown eyes and the fresh complexion of country youth, but those were her only assets in the way of good looks. 'You'll never be annoyed by people turning round in the street to have another look at you,' her mother had often told her, and sometimes, if Laura looked dashed, she would add: 'But that cuts both ways: if you're no beauty, be thankful you're not a freak.' So she had nothing to pride herself upon in that respect, and, being country born and with little education, she knew herself to be ignorant, and as to goodness, well, no one but herself knew how far she fell short of that so, rather than sink into nothingness in her own estimation, she chose to imagine herself interesting-looking.

Candleford Green was taking its afternoon nap when they arrived. The large irregular square of turf which gave the village its name was deserted but for one grazing donkey and a flock of geese which came cackling with outstretched necks towards the spring-cart to investigate. The children who at other times played there were in school and their fathers were at work in the fields, or in workshops, or at their different jobs in Candleford town. The doors of the row of shops which ran along one side of the green were open. A man in a white grocer's apron stood yawning and stretching his arms in one doorway, an old grey sheepdog slept in the exact middle of the road, the church clock chimed, then struck three, but those were the only signs of life, for it was Monday and the women of the place were too busy with their washing to promenade with their perambulators in front of the shops as on other afternoons.

On the farther, less-populated side of the green a white horse stood under a tree outside the smithy waiting its turn to be shod and, from within, as the spring-cart drew up, the ring of the anvil and the roar of the bellows could be heard.

Attached to the smithy was a long, low white house which might have been taken for an ordinary cottage of the more substantial kind but for a scarlet-painted letter-box let into the wall beneath a window at one end. Over the window was a painted board which informed the public that the building was CANDLEFORD GREEN POST AND TELEGRAPH OFFICE. At the other end of the building, above the door of the smithy, was another board which read: DORCAS LANE, SHOEING AND GENERAL SMITH.

Except for the sounds of the forge and the white horse dozing beneath the oak tree, that side of the green appeared even more somnolent than the shopping side. Their arrival had not been unobserved, however, for, as the cart drew up, a young smith darted from the forge and, seizing Laura's trunk, bore it away on his shoulder as if it weighed no more than a feather. 'Ma'am! The new miss has come,' they heard him call as he reached the back door of the house, and a moment later, the Post Office door-bell went *ping-ping* and Miss Lane herself stepped out to welcome her new assistant.

Miss Lane was not a tall woman and was slightly built, but an erect carriage, a commanding air, and the rustle as she walked of the rich silks she favoured gave her what was then known as a 'presence'. Bright, dark, almost black eyes were the only noticeable feature in her sallow but not otherwise unpleasing countenance. Ordinarily quietly observant, those eyes could disconcert with a flash of recognition of motives, sparkle with malice, or, more rarely, soften with sympathy. That afternoon, over a deep prune-coloured gown, she wore a small black satin apron embroidered almost to stiffness with jet beads, and, in accordance with fashion, her still luxurious black hair was plaited into a coronet above a curled fringe.

Not quite the Dorcas Lane, Shoeing and General Smith, that might have been expected after reading her signboard. Had she lived a century earlier or half a century later, she would probably have been found at the forge with a sledge-hammer in her hand for she had indomitable energy and a passion for doing and making things. But hers was an age when any work outside the four walls of a home was taboo for any woman who had any pretensions to refinement, and she had to content herself with keeping the books and attending to the correspondence of the old family business she had inherited. She had found one other outlet for her energy in her post office work, which also provided her with entertainment in the supervision of her neighbours' affairs and the study and analysis of their motives.

This may sound terrifying as now related, but there was nothing terrifying about Miss Lane. She kept the secrets with which she was entrusted in the course of her official duties most honourably, and if she laughed at some of her customers' foibles she laughed secretly. 'Clever' was the general village description of her. 'She's a clever one, that Miss Lane, as sharp as vinegar, but not bad in her way,' people would afterwards say to Laura. Only her two or three enemies said that if she had lived at one time she'd have been burned as a witch.

That afternoon she was in her most gracious mood. 'You've come just at the right time,' she said, kissing Laura. 'I've had a most terrible rush, half a dozen in at once for postal orders and what not, and the telegraph bell ringing like mad all the while. But it's over now, I think, for the time being, and the afternoon mail is not due for an hour, so come inside, do, both of you and we'll have a nice cup of tea before the evening's work begins.'

Laura experienced a slight shock when she heard of this recent pressure of business. How, she thought, would she ever be able to cope with such rushes. But she need not have feared: the rushes at Candleford Green Post Office existed chiefly in the imagination of the postmistress, who loved to make her office appear more busy and important than it was in reality.

Her father could not stay to tea, as he had his Candleford relations to visit, and Laura watched him drive away with the sinking feeling of one whose last link with a known world is vanishing. But, before the day was out, her childhood's life seemed long ago and far away to her, there was so much to see and hear and try to grasp in the new one.

As she followed her new employer through the little office and out to the big front living kitchen, the hands of the grandfather's clock pointed to a quarter to four. It was really only a quarter past three and the Post Office clock gave that time exactly, but the house clocks were purposely kept half an hour fast and meals and other domestic matters were timed by them. To keep thus ahead of time was an old custom in many country families which was probably instituted to ensure the early rising of man and maid in the days when five or even four o'clock was not thought an unreasonably early hour at which to begin the day's work. The smiths still began work at six and Zillah, the maid, was downstairs before seven, by which time Miss Lane and, later, Laura, was also up and sorting the morning mail.

The kitchen was a large room with a flagstone floor and two windows beneath which stood a long, solid-looking table large enough to accommodate the whole household at mealtimes. The foreman and three young unmarried smiths lived in the house, and each of these had his own place at table. Miss Lane, in a higher chair than the others, known as a carving-chair, sat enthroned at the head of the table, then, on the side facing the windows, came Laura and Matthew, the foreman, with a long space of tablecloth between them supposed to be reserved for visitors. Laura's seeming place of honour had, no doubt, been allotted to her for handiness in passing cups and plates. The young smiths sat three abreast at the bottom end of the table and Zillah, the maid, had a small side-table of her own. All meals excepting tea were taken in this order.

Cooking and washing-up were done in the back kitchen; the front kitchen was the family living- and dining-room. In the fireplace a small sitting-room grate with hobs had replaced the fire on the hearth of a few years before; but the open chimney and chimney-corners had been left, and from one of these a long, high-backed settle ran out into the room. In the space thus enclosed a red-and-black carpet had been laid to accommodate Miss Lane's chair at the head of the table and a few fireside chairs. This little room within a room was known as the hearthplace. Beyond it the stone floor was bare but for a few mats.

Brass candlesticks and a brass pestle and mortar ornamented the high mantelshelf, and there were brass warming-pans on the walls, together with a few coloured prints; one of the first man in this country to carry an umbrella – rain was coming down in sheets and he was followed by a jeering but highly ornamental crowd. A blue-and-white dish of oranges stuck with cloves stood upon the dresser. They were dry and withered at that time of the year, but still contributed their quota to the distinctive flavour of the air.

Everything there was just as Miss Lane had inherited it. Except for a couple of easy chairs by the hearth, she had added nothing. 'What was good enough for my parents and grandparents is good enough for me,' she would say when some of her more fashionable friends tried to persuade her to bring her house up to date. But family loyalty was rather an excuse than a reason for her preference; she kept the old things she had inherited because she enjoyed seeing and owning them.

That afternoon, when Laura arrived, a little round table in the hearthplace had already been laid for tea. And what a meal! There were boiled new-laid eggs and scones and honey and home-made jam and, to crown all, a dish of fresh Banbury cakes. The carrier had a standing order to bring her a dozen of those cakes every market day.

It seemed a pity to Laura that the first time she had been offered two eggs at one meal she could barely eat one and that the Banbury cake, hitherto to her a delicious rarity only seen in her home when purchased by visiting aunts, should flake and crumble almost untasted upon her plate because she felt too excited and anxious to eat. But Miss Lane ate enough for the two of them. Food was her one weakness. She loaded her scone, already spread with fresh farm butter, with black currant jam and topped it with cream while she inquired about the health of Laura's mother and told Laura what her new duties would be. Once or twice during tea the Post Office door-bell tinkled and she wiped her mouth and sailed majestically off to sell stamps, but the hour of her early tea was the quietest hour of the day; after that what she called her 'rush hour' began, and for that Laura was allowed to accompany her.

With what expert speed Miss Lane stamped letters and made up the mail, and with what ceremonious courtesy she answered questions which sounded like conundrums to Laura, was a wonder to hear and see.

The door-bell tinkled all the time as people came in to collect their afternoon mail. There was a delivery of letters in the morning, and the poorer inhabitants of the place only called in the afternoon when they were expecting a letter. 'I s'pose there isn't nothing for me, Miss Lane?' they would say almost apologetically, and would look pleased or disappointed according to her reply. Those of more assured position called regularly and these often would not speak at all, but put their heads inside the door and raise their eyebrows inquiringly. None of them gave their names or addresses, because Miss Lane knew everybody on and around the green and she seldom had to look in the pigeon-holes labelled 'A' to 'Z', because she had sorted the letters and could answer from memory. She often knew from whom the letter was expected and what its contents were likely to be and would console the disappointed callers with: 'Better luck in the morning. There's barely time for an answer as yet.'

Out in the kitchen Zillah and the workmen were at tea. The rattle of their teacups and the subdued hum of their conversation could be heard in the office. This was the only meal of the day at which Miss Lane herself did not preside. Zillah poured out, but she did not occupy her mistress's seat at the head of the table – that was sacred; between each pouring out she retired to her own seat on the settle with her own little table before her. At the other, more formal, meals, the conversation was carried on by Miss Lane and her foreman, with an occasional reference to Zillah when any item of local interest was under discussion, while the young smiths at the foot of the table munched in silence. At tea, with the mistress engaged elsewhere, there was more freedom, and sometimes Zillah's shrill laughter would break through a chorus of guffaws from the younger workmen. In moderation this was tolerated, but one day, when some one rapped loudly upon the table with a teacup and said (Miss Lane said 'shouted'), 'Another pint, please, landlady!' the office door opened and a voice as severe as that of a school-mistress admonishing her class called for 'Less noise there, please!'

None of them resented being spoken to like children, nor did the young journeymen resent being placed below the salt, nor Zillah at her separate table. To them these things were all part of an established order. To that unawakened generation freedom was of less account than good food, and of that in that household there was an abundance.

Tea was not considered a substantial meal. It was for the workmen, as Miss Lane counted time, an innovation. She could remember when bread and cheese and beer were at that hour taken to the forge for the men to consume standing. 'Afternoon bavour,' they had called it. Now a well-covered table awaited them indoors. Each man's plate was stacked with slices of bread and butter, and what was called 'a relish' was provided. 'What can we give the men for a relish at tea-time?' was an almost daily question in that household. Sometimes a blue-and-white basin of boiled new-laid eggs would be placed on the table. Three eggs per man was the standard allowance, but two or three extra were usually cooked 'in case', and at the end of the meal the basin was always empty. On other afternoons there would be brawn, known locally as 'collared head', or soused herrings, or a pork pie, or cold sausages.

As the clock struck five the scraping of iron-tipped boots would be heard and the men, with leather aprons wound up around their waists, and their faces, still moist from their visit to the pump in the yard, looking preternaturally clean against their work-soiled clothes, would troop into the kitchen. While they ate they would talk of the horses they had been shoeing. 'That new grey o' Squire's wer' as near as dammit to nippin' my ear. A groom ought'r stand by and hold th' young devil' or 'Poor old Whitefoot! About time he wer' pensioned off. Went to sleep an' nearly fell down top of me today, he did. Let's see, how old is he now, do you reckon?' 'Twenty, if he's a day. Mus' Elliott's father used to ride him to hounds and he's bin dead this ten 'ears. But you leave old Whitefoot alone. He'll drag that station cart for another five 'ears. What's he got to cart? Only young Jim, and he's a seven-stunner, if that, and maybe a bit of fish and a parcel or two. No, you take my word for't, old Whitefoot ain't going to die while he can see anybody else alive.' Or they would talk about the weather or the crops or some new arrival in the place, extracting the last grain of interest from every trifling event, while, separated from them by only a closed door, the new activities of a more sophisticated day were beginning.

On her first day in the office, Laura stood awkwardly by Miss Lane, longing to show her willingness to help, but not knowing how to begin. Once, when there was a brisk demand for penny stamps and the telegraph bell was ringing, she tried timidly to sell one, but she was pushed gently aside, and afterwards it was explained to her that she must not so much as handle a letter or sell a stamp until she had been through some mysterious initiation ceremony which Miss Lane called being 'sworn in'. This had to take place before a Justice of the Peace, and it had been arranged that she should go the next morning to one of the great houses in the locality for that purpose. And she would have to go alone, for until she herself had qualified, Miss Lane could not leave home during office hours, and she feared she would not know which doorbell to ring or what to say when she came into the great man's presence. Oh dear! this new life seemed very complicated.

The dread of this interview haunted her until, at Miss Lane's suggestion, she went out for a turn in the garden, where, she was told, she might always go for a breath of fresh air between busy times in the office. She had been in that garden before, but never in May, with the apple-blossom out and the wallflowers filling the air with their fragrance.

Narrow paths between high, built-up banks supporting flower borders, crowded with jonquils, auriculas, forget-me-nots and other spring flowers, led from one part of the garden to another. One winding path led to the earth closet in its bower of nut-trees half-way down the garden, another to the vegetable garden and on to the rough grass plot before the beehives. Between each section were thick groves of bushes with ferns and capers and Solomon's seal, so closed in that the long, rough grass there was always damp. Wasted ground, a good gardener might have said, but delightful in its cool, green shadiness.

Nearer the house was a portion given up entirely to flowers, not growing in beds or borders, but crammed together in an irregular square, where they bloomed in half-wild profusion. There were rose bushes there and lavender and rosemary and a bush apple-tree which bore little red and yellow streaked apples in later summer, and

Michaelmas daisies and red-hot pokers and old-fashioned pompom dahlias in autumn and peonies and pinks already budding.

An old man in the village came one day a week to till the vegetable garden, but the flower garden was no one's especial business. Miss Lane herself would occasionally pull on a pair of wash-leather gloves and transplant a few seedlings; Matthew would pull up a weed or stake a plant as he passed, and the smiths, once a year, turned out of the shop to dig between the roots and cut down dead canes. Betweenwhiles the flowers grew just as they would in crowded masses, perfect in their imperfection.

Laura, who came from a district often short of water, was amazed to find no less than three wells in the garden. There was the well beneath the pump near the back door which supplied the house with water; a middle well outside the inner smithy door used only for trade purposes, and what was called the 'bottom well' near the beehives. The bottom well was kept padlocked. Moss grew on its lid and nettles around it. At one time it had supplied the house with drinking water, but that was a long time ago.

Every one in any way connected with the place knew the story of the wells. No one had suspected the existence of the one near the house until, one day, while Miss Lane was still a small child, a visitor who had come to tea was on her way to what was still known as 'the little house' half-way down the garden. When she had gone a few yards from the back door a flagstone on the path gave way beneath her feet and she found herself slipping into a chasm. Fortunately, she was a substantially built woman and, by flinging out her arms, she was able to support her upper part above ground while her legs dangled in space. Her screams soon brought assistance and she was hauled to safety, and, the modern treatment of bed and hot-water bottles for shock being as yet undiscovered, Miss Lane's mother did what she could by well lacing the patient's tea with rum, which remedy acted so well that, when passing her cup a third time, she actually giggled and said: 'This tastes a lot better than that old well water'd have done!'

When or why the well had been abandoned and not properly filled in no one ever knew. Miss Lane's grandparents had had no knowledge of it, and they had come to live there early in the century and both they and her parents and herself as a child had walked gaily over it thousands of times, little suspecting the danger that lurked below. However, all ended well. After the well had been thoroughly cleansed and the water tested, it provided an excellent supply close at hand for the house.

When Laura went to bed that night in her new little bedroom with its pink-washed walls, faded chintz curtains, and chest of drawers all for her own use, she was too tired to write more in her new journal than: 'Came to live at Candleford Green today, Monday.' After she was in bed she heard Zillah call the cat, then plod, flat-footed, upstairs. Then the men came up, pad-padding in their stockinged feet, and, last of all, Miss Lane tap-tapping on her high heels.

Laura sat up in bed and drew aside the window curtain. Not a light to be seen, only darkness, thick and moist and charged with the scent of damp grass and cottage garden flowers. All was silent except for the sharp, sudden swish of a breeze in the smithy tree, and so it would be all night unless the hoof-sounds of a galloping horse rang out, followed by the pealing of the doctor's bell. There was no ordinary night traffic on country roads in those days.

II

On Her Majesty's Service

The interview next morning did not turn out so terrifying as Laura had expected. Sir Timothy smiled very kindly upon her when the footman ushered her into his Justice Room, saying: 'The young person from the Post Office, please, Sir Timothy.'

'What have you been up to? Poaching, rick-burning, or petty larceny?' he asked when the footman had gone. 'If you're as innocent as you look, I shan't give you a long sentence. So come along,' and he drew her by the elbow to the side of his chair. Laura smiled dutifully, for she knew by the twinkle of his keen blue eyes beneath their shaggy white eyebrows that Sir Timothy was joking.

As she leaned forward to take up a pen with which to sign the thick blue official document he was unfolding, she sensed the atmosphere of jollity, good sense, and good nature, together with the smell of tobacco, stables, and country tweeds he carried around like an aura.

'But read it! Read!' he cried in a shocked voice. 'Never put your name to anything before you have read it or you'll be signing your own death warrant one of these days.' And Laura read out, as clearly as her shyness permitted, the Declaration which even the most humble candidate for Her Majesty's Service had in those serious days to sign before a magistrate.

'I do solemnly promise and declare that I will not open or delay or cause or suffer to be opened or delayed any letter or anything sent by the post', it began, and went on to promise secrecy in all things.

When she had read it through, she signed her name. Sir Timothy signed his, then folded the document neatly for her to carry back to Miss Lane, who would send it on to the higher authorities.

Sir Timothy could not have been very busy that morning, for he kept her talking a long time, asking her age and where she came from and how many brothers and sisters she had and what she had learnt at school and if she thought she would like the post office business. 'You've been well brought up,' he said at last, as weightily as if pronouncing sentence in Court. 'And you should do well. Miss Lane is an excellent woman – most efficient, and kind, too, to those of whom she approves, though I should not like to offend her myself. By gad! I should not! I remember one day when she was a girl – but perhaps I had better not tell you that story. Now, I expect you would be glad of some refreshment. Ask Purchase, or Robert, to show you the way to the housekeeper's room. There's sure to be tea or coffee or something going there at this time,' and Laura dropped a little curtsey as she said 'No, thank you, Sir Timothy. No, thank you,' and passed through the door which he courteously held open and down the long resounding stone passage which led to the side door, and was very glad that she saw no one, for when she arrived the footman had teasingly pulled her hair and asked for a kiss.

Out in the park, she turned and looked back at the long, white, battlemented façade of the mansion, with its terraces, fountains and flower-beds, and thought: 'Thank goodness that's over. I don't suppose I shall ever see this place again.' But she erred in her supposition. She was to cross the park, come clanging through the iron swing gate, and pass beneath the tall, rook-noisy elms to the mansion every morning in all weathers for nearly three years.

For the first few days Laura feared she would never learn her new duties. Even in that small country Post Office there was in use what seemed to her a bewildering number and variety of official forms, to all of which Miss Lane who loved to make a mystery of her work referred by number, not name. But soon, in actual practice, 'AB/35', 'K.21', 'X.Y.13', or what not became 'The blue Savings Bank Form', 'The Postal Order Abstract', 'The Cash Account Sheet' and so on, and Laura found herself flicking them out of their pigeon-holes and carrying them without a moment's hesitation to where Miss Lane sat doing her accounts at the kitchen table.

Then the stamps! The 1d. and ½d. ones she already knew by sight were in 10s. and 5s. sheets which hot, nervous hands were inclined to tear, and those of higher value, neatly hinged in a cardboard-leaved book, ready to be sold for parcels and telegrams, had to be detached just so, working up from the left-hand bottom corner. And the cash drawer, with its three wooden bowls for gold, silver, and copper, and all three bowls at least half full, even the one for sovereigns and half-sovereigns! What a lot of money there must be in the world! Laura would run her fingers through the shining gold coins when the cash was counted at night and placed in the black japanned box ready to be taken upstairs, wrapped in an old woolly shawl as disguise, and stood on the top shelf of Miss Lane's clothes cupboard. Occasionally there was a banknote in the japanned box, but no Treasury notes, for there were none issued; there was plenty of gold to serve as currency in those days. Gold in plenty flowed through the country in a stream, but a stream to which only the fortunate had access. One poor half-sovereign was doled out on Saturday night to the lowest-paid workers; men who had a trade might get a whole sovereign and a few pieces of silver.

At first, when giving change, Laura boggled and hesitated and counted again, but although she had learned little arithmetic at school she was naturally quick at figures, and that part of her work soon became easy to her. And she liked seeing and speaking and being spoken to by the post office customers, especially the poorer ones, who would tell her about their affairs and sometimes ask her advice. The more important at first would ignore her if Miss Lane was present, or, if she was absent, would ask to see her; but they soon got used to seeing a new face there, and once, when Laura had gone indoors to tea, a gentleman farmer from a neighbouring hamlet actually inquired what had become of 'that charmin' young gal you've got now'. That set the seal of acceptance upon her and, fortunately, it was the only compliment so definitely expressed. Further inquiries of the kind might not have pleased Miss Lane. She liked Laura and was glad to find she was giving satisfaction, but naturally expected to stand first in her customers' regards.

Working hours in such small post offices as that where Laura was employed were then from the arrival of the seven o'clock morning mail till the office was closed at night, with no weekly half-day off and Sunday not entirely free, for there was a Sunday morning delivery of letters and an outward mail to be made up in the evening. Slave's hours, she was told by those employed directly by Government in the larger post offices, where they worked an eight-hour day. And so they would have been had life moved at its present-day pace. At that time life moved in a more leisurely manner; the amount of business transacted in such village post offices was smaller and its nature more simple, there were no complicated forms with instructions for filling in to be dealt out to the public, no Government allowances to be paid, and the only pensions were the quarterly ones to ex-Service men, of whom there would not be more than three or four in such a place. During the day there were long, quiet intervals in which meals could be taken in comparative peace, or reading or knitting were possible, while where two were engaged in the business, as at Candleford Green, there were opportunities of getting out into the fresh air.

Most important of all, there was leisure for human contacts. Instead of rushing in a crowd to post at the last moment, villagers would stroll over the green in the afternoon to post their letters and stay for a chat, often bringing an apple or a pear or a nose-gay from their gardens for Laura. There was always at least one pot of cut flowers in the office, pink moss-roses, sweet williams and lad's love in summer, and in autumn the old-fashioned yellow-and-bronze button chrysanthemums which filled cottage gardens at that time.

In time Laura came to know these regular customers well. Some letter or telegram they had received or were sending opened the way to confidences and often, afterwards, she was treated as an old friend and would ask if the daughter in Birmingham had made a good recovery from her confinement, or if the son in Australia was having better luck, or how the wife's asthma was, or if the husband had succeeded in getting the job he was trying for. And they would ask Laura if her people at home were well or compliment her upon a new cotton frock she was wearing, or ask her if she liked such-and-such a flower, because they had some at home they could bring her.

The morning mail arrived from the head office by walking post-man at seven o'clock, and it was Laura's first duty of the day to attend to the opening of the mail-bag and the distribution of its contents in what had in times past been one of the numerous out-buildings of the house, wash-house, brew house, or pantry. New-floored and new-ceiled and with sorting-benches placed around, it made a convenient little sorting office, although, with no other means of heating than an oil stove, it was cold there in winter.

Every morning, the postman who had brought the mail remained to sort out his own letters for the village delivery, and the two women letter-carriers who did cross-country deliveries to outlying houses and farms had their own sorting. The elder woman, Mrs Gubbins, was an old country-woman who wore for her round a lilac sunbonnet with apron and shawl. She was a crabbed old creature who seldom spoke beyond grunting a 'Good morning', except when some local scandal was afoot, when she could be voluble enough. The other postwoman was still in her thirties and as pleasant in manner as Mrs Gubbins was uncouth. Her name was Mrs Macey, and more will be told about her later.

The morning postman, Thomas Brown, was a stockily built man with greying hair, who had, as far as was known always led a quiet, respectable life. Until recently he had taken great interest in local affairs and had had such good judgement that he had occasionally been asked to arbitrate in local disputes. A teetotaller and a non-smoker, his only known vice had been an addiction to grumbling, especially about the weather, which, he seemed convinced, was ordered by some one with a special grudge against postmen.

Then, just before Laura knew him, he had been converted at a chapel revivalist meeting and the people who had formerly lain in wait for him on his round to ask his advice about their worldly affairs – what, for instance, could they ask from the MFH for those three hens that old fox'd carried off in the night, or for the cabbage patch the hunt had trampled – now almost ran in the opposite direction when they saw him coming, lest he should ask impertinent questions about their souls. 'How is it with your soul?' he would unblushingly inquire of any chance-met acquaintance, or, more directly, 'Have you found salvation?' and, in face of a question like that, what could a man or woman do but mumble and look silly?

All but Miss Lane, who, suddenly asked in an earnest tone, 'Miss Lane, are you a Christian?' replied haughtily, 'I do not see that whether I am or not is any business of yours, but, if you particularly want to know, I am a Christian in the sense that I live in a Christian country and try to order my life according to Christian teaching. Dogma I leave to those better qualified than myself to expound, and I advise you to do the same.'

That last was a shrewd thrust, because he had recently become a local preacher, but he did not feel it as such, for he only shook his grey head and said mournfully, 'Ah, I see you've not found Christ yet.'

Laura was pleased when she heard that his wife had been converted, for, outside his home, he found little sympathy. His position seemed to her quite clear. He had found, as he thought, a priceless treasure which all mankind might share if they would, and he wanted to make it known to them. The pity was that he himself was so poor an advertisement of the change of heart he wished them to experience. His expression and voice when he spoke of Divine Love failed to light up or to soften, and, although he now declared that he had been the chief of sinners, his outward life had always been so exemplary that there could be no sudden change there to illustrate and enforce his new faith. Moreover, he was still grumbling and censorious.

But at least he had the courage of his convictions. Laura discovered that in him once when one of the higher officials was paying the office a visit of inspection. He was a very great man officially and had arrived, wearing a top-hat and an immaculate morning suit, in the station fly. When the office had been surveyed and a few criticisms made, none of them very severe, because the business was really well run and the delicious tea which followed the survey had softened the edges before they were delivered, he announced that he had to see Postman Brown, then about due with a letter-box collection. Laura, quietly sorting the night mail, could not help hearing what was said at this interview.

'About this new Sunday evening collection, now,' began the surveyor in his high-pitched, public-schoolboyish accent, 'I hear you object to doing it.'

Postman (subdued, but not intimidated): 'Yes, sir, I do object.'

Surveyor: 'On what grounds, may I ask? Your colleagues have agreed, and there is extra pay for it. It is your place, my man, to carry out the duties laid down for you by the Department, and I advise you for your own good to withdraw your objection immediately.'

Postman (firmly): 'I can't, sir.'

Surveyor: 'But why, man, why? What do you usually do on a Sunday evening? Got another job? Because, if so, I warn you that to undertake outside employment of any kind is against the regulations.'

Postman (manfully and with spirit): 'My job on Sunday evenings, sir, is to worship my Creator, who Himself laid down the law, "Keep holy the Sabbath Day", and I can't go against that, sir.'

By that time the man was trembling. He knew that his post and the pension he had so nearly earned hung in the balance. He drew out a big red, white-spotted handkerchief and mopped his forehead. Yet there was still a certain dignity about him far removed from his ordinary demeanour.

The gentleman appeared to less advantage. His easy, urbane, authoritative manner dropped from him, and there was an ugly sneer in the way he pronounced the words: 'Takes a lot out of you, I suppose, this worshipping business! Better attend to the work which provides you with bread and butter. But you can go now. I will report what you have said and you will hear further about it.' Then, to Laura, as Brown went out with a humble 'Good night, sir': 'A cantankerous man. I know his kind. Out to make trouble. But he will find he will have to fit in the Sunday evening work with his psalm-singing.'

But, although highly placed, it appeared that Mr Cochrane was not all powerful. Some one at headquarters was more sympathetically disposed to Sabbatarian principles, or perhaps the head postmaster, who was a bit of a psalm-singer himself, interceded for Brown, for, after a few weeks of suspense, he was excused Sunday evening attendance. The other postmen did his collection with pleasure, for it brought them in a little extra pay, and he continued to add to his already high weekly walking mileage by tramping the countryside to preach in little local chapels.

Twice a year the head postmaster from Candleford came to audit the accounts and made a general survey of the office. This was officially supposed to be a surprise visit, with the object of detecting any shortage of cash or neglect of duty, but Mr Rushton and Miss Lane were on such terms that on the morning of the day of his intended visitation the head postmaster would himself come to the telegraph instrument and with his own hands signal to Laura: 'Please tell Miss Lane I shall be paying her a surprise visit this afternoon.'

That saved trouble all round. By the time Mr Rushton's pony-carriage drew up at the post office door, the account books, sheets of stamps, postal orders, licences, and so on, together with the cash, ready-counted in neat piles, would be arranged in readiness on the kitchen table. So the official business did not take long and, that dispatched, the occasion became a social one.

Tea was laid on the round table in the parlour for Mr Rushton's visits, with Miss Lane in her best silk, and a long gold chain twice round her neck and tucked into her waistband, pouring out tea from the best silver teapot, Mr Rushton doing full justice to the country fare (there was once cold duck on the table), and Laura bobbing in and out between her calls to the post office counter. The first time she was trusted to warm the pot and put in the tea from the special caddy for this function, she forgot to put in the tea and nearly dropped on the floor with nervous terror when the other two stared blankly at the crystal stream proceeding from the teapot.

After tea the garden and chickens and pigs had to be surveyed and the pony-cart loaded up with country produce, including a huge, old-fashioned bouquet of flowers for Mrs Rushton.

It was an old-fashioned way of conducting business and Mr Rushton was an old-fashioned postmaster. He was a neat, middle-aged little man, very precise in his speech and manner, and with what many considered an exaggerated sense of his own importance. Pleasant, if somewhat patronizing to well-doers on his staff, but a terror to the careless and slipshod worker. He was under the impression that his own office staff adored him. 'The crew of my little ship', he would say when speaking of those under him, 'the crew of my little ship know who is captain.' It is sad to have to record that the crew in private spoke of their captain as 'Holy Joe'.

That was because in private life Mr Rushton was a pillar of the Methodist Connexion in Candleford town, Sunday School superintendent, occasional preacher, and the ready host of visiting ministers, a great man locally in his Church. Which perhaps accounted for his style of dress. In his black, or very dark grey clothes and round, black soft felt hat, driving his fat grey pony in the lanes, he might himself have been taken for a minister, or even for a clergyman of the Established Church. On his salary of at most two hundred and fifty a year, he was able in those spacious days to keep his own pony carriage, a maid for his wife, and to entertain his friends and educate his children.

He was liked by the Candleford townspeople, but with those in the big country houses he was not a favourite. They thought him a too pedantic stickler for official rules. 'That little jack-in-office', one of the squires called him, and there was a story of a fox-hunting baronet who had terminated an interview in the office marked 'Postmaster' by hurling a stone bottle of ink at the official head. It missed its mark, fortunately, but some of the younger clerks in his office still took a pride in pointing out the faint remaining traces of the splashes on the wallpaper.

At an early stage of their acquaintance, Mr Rushton promised Laura the offer of the next vacancy for a learner in his office. But the vacancy never occurred. His only two women clerks were the daughters of a minister, a friend of his own, and boarded with his family. They were quiet, refined, pleasant young women in the early thirties, of a type to which most women clerks in the post office at that time belonged. The 'young ladies' with the artificial pearls and bad manners belonged to the early years of this century and disappeared before the last war. In Laura's time post office employment was largely the preserve of ministers' and schoolmasters' daughters. It had not become popularized. The pay of a learner in the larger offices was very small, not nearly sufficient to live upon away from home, and the smaller offices, where learners were boarded, demanded a premium. Laura had crept in by a kind of back door and later she was sometimes reminded of that fact. 'Why should I teach you? My parents paid for me to learn' was a spirit not unknown in the service.

For some time Laura hoped one of the Miss Rapleys would marry; but neither of them showed the least disposition to oblige her in that manner, and gradually her hopes of a Candleford vacancy faded. And no other offered which it was possible for her to accept. This is no success story. She remained what was officially known as an assistant throughout her brief official career. But there were compensations, which might not have appealed to everybody, but appealed to her.

The telegraph instrument had been installed in the parlour, where its scientific-looking white dials and brass trimmings looked strikingly modern against Miss Lane's old rosewood and mahogany furniture. It was what was known as the ABC type of instrument, now long superseded even in such small offices by the telephone. But it served very well in its day, being easy to learn and reliable in working. Larger and busier offices had Sounder and Single Needle instruments, worked by the Morse code and read by sound. The ABC was read by sight. A handle, like that of a coffee mill, guided a pointer from letter to letter on a dial which had the alphabet printed around it, clockwise, and this came out and was read on a smaller dial at the other end of the circuit. Surrounding the operating dial were brass studs, or keys, one for each letter, and the operator, turning the handle with one hand, depressed the keys with the finger of the other, and by so doing spelt out the words of a telegram. A smaller dial above, known as the 'receiver', recorded incoming messages.

For a few days Laura, with a book propped open before her to supply the words, practised sending. Round and round went the handle and *blick, blick, blick*, went the keys, slowly and jerkily at first, then more smoothly and quickly. Sometimes a bell attached to the instrument would ring and a real telegram come through, which Miss Lane would take off while Laura tried hard to follow the pointer on the smaller, upper dial. It whirled round so madly that she feared her eyes would never be able to follow it, but, gradually, they became accustomed to note its brief pauses and in about a week she was able to take charge of the simple apparatus.

How to get the telegrams delivered promptly was one of Miss Lane's problems. A girl named Minnie, who lived in one of the cottages near, could usually be depended upon to do this if she happened to be at home; but although there were only about a dozen incoming telegrams a day on the average, they were apt to come in rushes with long intervals between, and often Minnie had barely had time to get out of hailing distance before another telegram arrived. Then there was running to and fro to find another messenger, or Zillah or the apprentice from the blacksmith's shop would be pressed into the service. Neither of these went willingly, and often they could ill be spared from their work, but it was a strict rule of the establishment that no telegram must be delayed. Another worrying thing about the delivery of telegrams was that even when two came fairly close together they were bound to be for addresses in opposite directions. Many were for farms or for country houses two or even three miles distant, and Minnie trailed many miles about the countryside in a day.

Trailing is the only way to describe her method of progress, for she had an apparently slow, languid walk which was, in fact, deceptive, as she managed to cover long distances and usually be back to time. She was a pretty, doll-faced country girl of fifteen, with wide, rather vacant-looking blue eyes and a great love of finery. She usually appeared at the office in a very clean, if sometimes old, print frock and a flower-wreathed hat. One very hot day in a very hot summer, Miss Lane brought forth from her hoard an old white silk parasol with a deep cream lace frill and presented it to Minnie. Her face as she went off beneath it to deliver her telegram wore an expression Laura never forgot. It was one of utter felicity.

Miss Lane's parlour door opened out into the public portion of the office and it sometimes happened that after attending to the telegraph instrument Laura found herself cut off from the inner side of the counter by what appeared to be a private and confidential conversation between Miss Lane and a customer. Then she would close the door softly and go straight to the bookcase. A few books, such as *Cooking and Household Management*, *The Complete Farrier*, and Dr Johnson's *Dictionary*, were kept on one of the kitchen window-seats, but all the best books were kept behind glass doors above the bureau in the parlour. When one of these was lent to Laura, it had first to be fitted with a brown-paper jacket, for Miss Lane was very particular about her books, most of which had belonged to her father.

The collection was an unusual one to be found in a tradesman's parlour at that time; but her father had been an unusual man, a lover of poetry, especially of Shakespeare, and a student of history and astronomy.

There were *The Works of William Shakespeare* in two large, flat volumes, and Hume's *History of England* in at least a dozen small fat ones, Scott's *Poetical Works* and a number of the Waverley Novels, Cowper's poems and Campbell's and Gray's, Thomson's *Seasons* and many other such books. Any of these, she was told, she might borrow; with one exception. That was Byron's *Don Juan*, a terrible book, she was told, and most unfit for her reading. 'I don't know why I haven't destroyed it long ago,' said Miss Lane. 'Next time there's a bonfire in the garden, I must see about it.'

Laura knew she ought to be, and was, ashamed of herself when, at every opportunity, she stood before the bookcase with goggling eyes and many a guilty glance at the door, devouring another half-canto of *Don Juan*. She slipped the book into her pocket one night and took it to read in bed and narrowly escaped detection when Miss Lane came suddenly into her room to give some instruction about the next morning's mail. She saved herself by tucking the book down into the bed beside her, but the feel of its sharp edges against her side made her so incoherent that Miss Lane glanced round suspiciously. 'No reading in bed, now,' she said. 'You've got no need to wear out your eyesight, and I'm sure I don't fancy being burnt to death in my sleep.' And Laura replied in a small, meek voice, 'No, Miss Lane.'

But she went on reading. She could not help it. How fascinating the book was! She felt she simply had to know what came next, and the blue skies and seas of those foreign shores and the seaside caves and golden sands and the wit of the author and the felicity of his language and the dexterity of his rhymes enchanted her. She was shocked by some of the hero's adventures, but more often thrilled. Laura learned quite a lot by reading *Don Juan*.

When she had finished eating that forbidden fruit, she turned to Shakespeare. Miss Lane said Shakespeare was the greatest poet who ever lived and vowed that when she had time she would re-read every one of the plays herself. But she never did. She had read them all at some time, probably to please her father, and still remembered the stories and a few lines here and there of the poetry. Sometimes, when she was in a good mood, Laura would begin: 'Good morrow, Father,' and she would reply, 'Benedicite. What early tongue so sweet saluteth me?' and go on being the Friar to Laura's Romeo. But much more often, in their off-duty hours, she was deep in *The Origin of Species*, or one of the books on human psychology she had bought at a doctor's sale of furniture. Such books as those and the leading articles in *The Times* were the kind of reading she liked. But, because of her father, she could understand Laura's love of quite other literature.

When Laura had read most of the parlour books, Miss Lane suggested that, as she was fond of reading, she should take out a library ticket at the Mechanics' Institute in Candleford town. Laura took out the ticket and, within a year, she had read and laughed and cried over the works of Charles Dickens, read such of the Waverley Novels as had not before come her way, and made the acquaintance of many other writers hitherto unknown to her. *Barchester Towers* and *Pride and Prejudice* gave her a taste for the work of Trollope and Jane Austen which was to be a precious possession for life.

The caretaker at the Institute acted as librarian during the day. He was a one-legged man named Hussey, and his manner and qualifications bore no resemblance to those of librarians today. He seemed to bear a positive grudge against frequent borrowers. 'Carn't y'make up y're mind?' he would growl at some lingerer at the shelves. 'Te-ak th' first one y'comes to. It won't be no fuller o' lies than t'others,' and, if that admonition failed, he would bring his broom and sweep close around the borrower's feet, not sparing toes or heels. Laura sometimes wondered if his surname was inherited from some virago of a maternal ancestor.

But there was no dearth of books. After she left home, Laura never suffered in that way. Modern writers who speak of the booklessness of the poor at that time must mean books as possessions; there were always books to borrow.

III

The Green

In Laura's time Candleford Green was still a village, and, in spite of its nearness to a small country town which was afterwards to annex it, the life lived there was still village life. And this, she soon discovered, was as distinct from that of a hamlet, such as that in which she had been bred, as the life of a country town was from that of a city.

In the hamlet there lived only one class of people; all did similar work, all were poor and all equal. The population of Candleford Green was more varied. It had a clergyman of its own and doctor and independent gentlewomen who lived in superior cottages with stabling attached, and artisans and labourers who lived in smaller and poorer ones, though none so small and poor as those of the hamlet. Then there were shopkeepers and the schoolmaster and a master builder and the villa people who lived on the new building estate outside the village, most of whom worked in Candleford town, a couple of miles away. The village was a little world in itself; the hamlet was but a segment.

In the large country houses around lived squires and baronets and lords who employed armies of indoor servants, gardeners, and estate workers. The village was their village, too: they attended its church, patronized its shops, and had influence upon its affairs. Their ladies might be seen, in mellow tweeds and squashed hats, going in and out of the shops in the morning, or bringing flowers with which to decorate the church for some festival, or popping into the village school to see that all was going on there as they thought it should be. In the afternoon, the same ladies in silks and satins and huge feather boas would pass through the village in their carriages, smiling and bowing to all they met, for it was part of their duty, as they conceived it, to know every inhabitant. Some of the older village women still curtsied in acknowledgement, but that pretty, old-fashioned if somewhat servile custom was declining, and with the younger, or more enlightened, or slightly higher socially, smiles and a jerk of the head by way of a bow had become the usual response.

Every member of the community knew his or her place and few wished to change it. The poor, of course, wished for higher wages, the shopkeepers for larger shops and quicker turnovers and the rich may have wished for higher rank and more extensive estates, but few wished to overstep the boundaries of class. Those at the top had no reason to wish for change and by others the social order was so generally accepted that there was no sense of injustice.

If the squire and his lady were charitable to the poor, affable to the tradesmen, and generous when writing out a cheque for some local improvement, they were supposed to have justified the existence of their class. If the shopkeeper gave good value and weight and reasonable credit in hard times, and the skilled workman had served his apprenticeship and turned out good work, no one grudged them their profits or higher wages. As to the labouring class, that was the most conservative of all. 'I know my place and I keep it,' some man or woman would say with a touch of pride in the voice, and if one of the younger and more spirited among them had ambition, those of their own family would often be the first to ridicule and discourage them.

The edifice of society as it then stood, apparently sound but already undermined, had served its purpose in the past. It could not survive in a changing world where machines were already doing what had been men's work and what had formerly been the luxuries of the few were becoming necessities of the many; but in its old age it had some pleasant aspects and not everything about it was despicable.

Along one side of the large oblong stretch of greensward which gave the village its name ran the road into Candleford town, a pleasant two miles, with its raised footpath and shady avenue of beech trees. Facing the road and the green on that side, shops and houses and garden walls were strung closely enough together to form a one-sided street. This was known as 'the best side of the green' and many who lived there complained of the Post Office having been established on the opposite, quieter side 'so out of the way and ill-convenient'. The Post Office side of the green was known as 'the dull side', but Miss Lane did not find it dull, for, from the vantage point of her windows, she had a good view of the more populous road and of all that was going on there.

The quieter road had only the Post Office and the smithy and one tall old red-brick Georgian farmhouse where, judging by its size and appearance, people of importance must once have lived, but where then only an old cowman and his wife occupied one corner. The windows of their rooms had white lace curtains and pot plants; the other windows stared blankly in long rows out on the green. Rumour said that on certain nights of the year ghostly lights might be seen passing from window to window of the upper storey, for the house was supposed to be haunted, as all unoccupied or partly occupied large houses were supposed to be at that date. But old Cowman Jollife and his wife laughed at these stories and declared that they were too cosy in their own rooms on winter nights to go looking for ghosts in the attics. 'Us knows when we be well off,' John would say, 'wi' three good rooms rent-free, an' milk an' taties found; we ain't such fools as to go ferritin' round for that which might fritten us away!'

Between these few buildings on the quiet side were rickyard and orchard and garden walls with lilacs, laburnums, and fruit trees overhanging. This greenery with the golden or dun thatch of the pointed-topped ricks and the sights and sounds of the farmyard and smithy gave this side of the green a countrified air which some of the more go-ahead spirits of the place resented. They said the land occupied by the gardens and orchards ought to be developed. There was room there for a new Baptist chapel and a row of good shops, and these would bring more trade to the place and encourage people to build more houses. But, for a few more years, the dull side of the green was to remain as it was. The farmyard sounds of cock-crow and milking-time and the *tang, tang* of the forge were to blend with the strains of gramophone music and the hooting of motor horns before the farmhouse was demolished and its stock driven farther afield and the smithy gave place to an up-to-date motor garage with petrol pumps and advertisement hoardings.

Except for the church and vicarage, which stood back among trees at one end of the green with only the church tower showing, and roomy old inn which had known coaching days and now, after a long eclipse, was beginning to call itself an hotel, at the other, these two roads were almost all there was of the village. There were labourers' cottages out in the fields and a group of these called 'Hungry End' stood just outside the village at the farther end, and there was the new building estate on the Candleford road, but neither of these was included in the view from the Post Office.

Between the two roads lay the green with its daisies and dandelions and grazing donkey and playing children and old men sunning themselves on the two backless benches: or, in rainy weather, deserted but for a few straggling figures crossing from various angles with umbrellas and letters to post in their hands.

The road past the shops was the favourite promenade and meeting place, but on a few occasions the green itself became the focus of attention, and the greatest of these was when, on the morning of the first Saturday in January, the Hunt met there in front of the roomy old inn. Then riders in scarlet would rein in their mounts to reach down for a stirrup-cup, and their ladies, in tight-fitting habits with long, flowing skirts, would turn on their side-saddles to wave their hunting-crops to their friends, or gather in groups to gossip while their mounts backed and fidgeted, and the waving white sterns of the pack moved hither and thither in massed formation at the word of command of the Huntsman, there known as the whipper-in. If one of the hounds strayed a yard, he would call it by name: 'Hi, Minnie!' or Spot, or Cowslip, or Trumpeter, and the animal would look lovingly into his face as it turned in meek obedience, which always seemed wonderful to Laura, in view of the fact that within a few hours the same animal might be helping to tear a living fellow creature limb from limb.

But few there thought of the fox, beyond hoping that the first covert would be successfully drawn and that the day's sport would be good.

The whole neighbourhood turned out to see the Meet. Both roadways were lined with little low basketwork pony-carriages with elderly ladies in furs, governess-cars with nurses and children, farm carts with forks stuck upright in loads of manure, and butcher's and grocer's carts and baker's white-tilted vans, and donkey-barrows in which red-faced, hoarse-shouting hawkers stood up for a better view. Matthew used to say that it was a funny thing that everybody's errand led them in that direction on Meet Morning.

On the green itself school-teachers, curates, men in breeches and gaiters with ash sticks, men in ragged coats and mufflers, smartly dressed girls from Candleford town, and local women in white aprons with babies in their arms pressed forward to see all there was to be seen, while older children rushed hither and thither shouting, 'Tally-ho! Tally-ho!' and only missed by a miracle being hit by the horses' hoofs.

Every year, as soon as the Meet had assembled, Matthew would hang up his leather apron, slip into his second-best coat, and say that he must just pop across the green for a moment; Squire, or Sir Austin, or Muster Ramsbottom of Pilvery had asked him to run his hand over his mare's fetlock. But the smiths were to get on with their work, none of their 'gaping an' gazing', they had seen 'osses before and them that rode on 'em though to judge by some of their doings you'd think they didn't know the near from the off side.

As soon as he had disappeared, the smiths left anvil and tools and forge and fire to take care of themselves and hurried out to a little hillock a few yards from the smithy door, where they stood close-packed with their fringed leather aprons flapping about their legs.

No one was likely to have business at the Post Office counter that morning, but the telegraph instrument had to be attended to, and, although that was furnished with a warning bell which could be heard all over the house, both Miss Lane and Laura found it necessary to be in constant attendance.

From the window near the instrument the green, with its restive horses and swaying crowds, its splashes of scarlet coats and its white splash of hounds, could be viewed in comfort. Miss Lane could recognize at sight almost every one there and give little character sketches of many for Laura's benefit. That gentleman there on the tall grey was 'out-running the constable'; he had got through a fortune of so much in so many years and was now in 'queer street'. The very horse he sat upon did not belong to him; he had got it to try out, as she happened to know; Tom Byles, the vet, had told her only yesterday. And that lady there with the floating veil was a perfect madam; just look at all those men around her, did you ever, now! And that pretty quiet little thing was a cousin of Sir Timothy's, and that fine, handsome young fellow was only a farmer.

'Poor young things!' she said one day when a man and a girl rider had, ostensibly to soothe the restlessness of their mounts, detached themselves from the main body of the Hunt and were riding at a walking pace backwards and forwards before the Post Office windows. 'Poor young things, trying to get in a word together. Think they are alone, no doubt, and them with the eyes of all the field upon them. Ah, I thought so! Here comes her mother. It'll never do, my poor dears, it'll never do, with him a younger son without a penny to bless himself, as the saying goes.'

But Laura, as yet, had less sympathy with lovers. Her eyes were fixed on a girl of about her own age in a scarlet coat and a small black velvet jockey cap, whose pony was giving her trouble. A groom came up quickly and took its reins. Laura thought she would like to be dressed like that girl and to ride to hounds across fields and over streams on that mild January morning. In imagination she saw herself flying across a brook, *her* hair streaming and *her* gloved hands holding the reins in such a masterly fashion that other riders near called out 'Well done!' as she had heard riders near her home call out when witnessing a feat of horsemanship.

When the Hunt moved off to draw the appointed cover, men and women and boys and girls would follow on foot as long as their breath lasted. Two or three working men of the tougher kind would follow the Hunt all day, pushing through thorn hedges and leaping or wading brooks, ostensibly on the chance of earning a sixpence or two for opening gates for the timid or pointing out directions to the lagging horsemen; but, actually, for the fun of the sport, which they thought well worth the loss of a day's pay and a good dressing down by the Mis'is when they got home torn and tired and hungry at night.

In summer what grass there was on the green was cut with the scythe by the man who owned the donkey which grazed there. It is doubtful if he had any legal right to the grass, but even if not, his gain in donkey fodder was well repaid to the community by the newly cut hay scent which seemed to hang about the village all the summer. One of Laura's most lasting impressions of Candleford Green was that of leaning out of her bedroom window one soft, dark summer night when the air was full of new-made hay and elderflower scents. It could not have been late in the evening, for a few dim lights still showed on the opposite side of the green and some boy or youth, on his way home, was whistling 'Annie Laurie'. Laura felt she could hang there for ever, drinking in the soft, scented night air.

One other scene she remembered at the time of year when it is still summer, but the evenings are closing in. Then youths were on the green flying kites on which they had contrived to fix lighted candle-ends. The little lights floated and flickered like fireflies against the dusk of the sky and the darker tree-tops. It was a pretty sight, although, perhaps, the sport was a dangerous one, for one of the kites caught fire and came down as tinder. At that, some men, drinking their pints outside the inn door for coolness, rushed forward and put a stop to it. Madness, they called it, stark staring madness, and asked the youths if they wanted to set the whole place on fire. But how innocent and peaceful compared with our present menace from the air!

Those who did not care for the dull side of the green would point with pride to the march of progress on the opposite side. To the fine new plate-glass window at the grocer's; the plaster-of-paris model of a three-tiered wedding cake which had recently appeared among the buns and scones at the baker's next door; and the fishmonger's where, to tell the truth, after the morning orders for the big houses had gone out, the principal exhibits were boxes of bloaters. But how many villages had a fishmonger at all? And the corner shop, known as the 'Stores', where the latest (Candleford Green) fashions might be studied. Only the butcher lagged behind. His shop stood back in a garden, and the lambs and hares and legs of mutton behind its one small window were framed in roses and honeysuckle.

Interspersing the shops were houses; one, a long, low brown one where Doctor Henderson lived. His red lamp, when lighted at night, made a cheerful splash of colour. Less appreciated by those who lived near was the disturbing peal of his night bell followed by some anxious voice bawling up to him through the speaking-tube. Some of his night calls came from outlying hamlets and farms, six, eight, or even ten miles distant, and those from the poor had to be brought on foot, for bicycles were still rare and the telephone was, as yet, unknown there.

The doctor, dragged from his warm bed at midnight, had often to saddle or harness his own horse before he could start on his long ride or drive, for even if he kept a man to drive him around in the day time, that man might not be available for night work. And yet, swear as he might, and often did, on the journey, damning horse, messenger, roads, and weather, the doctor brought cheer and skill and kindness to his patient's bedside.

'She'll be all right now our doctor's come,' the women downstairs would say, 'and he's that cheerful he's making her laugh between her pains. "That's my fifth cup of tea," he says. "If I have any more" – but I'd better not say what he said'd happen – only it made Maggie laugh and she can't be so bad if she's laughing.' And that was said of a man who, after a hard day's work, had been dragged from his bed to spend the night in a tiny, fireless bedroom overseeing a difficult delivery.

Laura's mother used to say, 'All doctors are heroes', and she spoke feelingly, for the night before Laura was born the doctor came from the nearest town through one of the worst snowstorms in then living memory. He had to leave his horse and gig at a farmhouse on the main road and walk the last mile, for the by-road to the hamlet was blocked to wheeled traffic by drifts. No wonder he said when Laura at last put in an appearance: 'There you are! Here is the person who has caused all this bother. Let us hope she will prove worth it!' Which saying was kept as a rod in pickle to be repeated to Laura when she misbehaved during her childhood.

From her Post Office window in summer, Laura could see the grey church tower with its flagstaff and the twisted red-brick chimneys of the Vicarage rising out of massed greenery. In winter, when the trees were bare, there were glimpses of the outer tracery of the east window of the church and the mellow brick front of the Vicarage with rooks tumbling and cawing above the high elm-tops where they nested in early spring.

At the time when Laura arrived at Candleford Green a clergyman of the old type held the cure of souls of its inhabitants. He was an elderly man with what was then known as a fine presence, being tall and large rather than stout, with rosy cheeks, a lion-like mane of white hair, and an air of conscious authority. His wife was a dumpy little roly-poly of a woman who wore old, comfortable clothes about the village because, as she was once heard to say, 'Everybody here knows who I am, so why bother about dress?' For church and for afternoon calls upon her equals, she dressed in the silks and satins and ostrich feathers befitting her rank as the granddaughter of an earl and the wife of a vicar with large private means. She was said by the villagers to be 'a bit managing', but, on the whole, she was popular with them. When visiting the cottagers or making purchases at the shops, she loved to hear and discuss the latest tit-bit of gossip, which she was not above repeating – some said with additions.

The church services were long, old-fashioned and dull, but all was done decently and in order, and the music and singing were exceptionally good for a village church at that date. Mr Coulsdon preached to his poorer parishioners contentment with their divinely appointed lot in life and submission to the established order of earthly things. To the rich, the responsibilities of their position and their obligations in the way of charity. Being rich and highly placed in the little community and genuinely loving a country life, he himself naturally saw nothing wrong in the social order, and, being of a generous nature, the duty of helping the poor and afflicted was also a pleasure to him.

In cold, hard winters soup was made twice a week in the vicarage washing-copper, and the cans of all comers were filled without question. It was soup that even the very poor – connoisseurs from long and varied experience of charity soups – could find no fault with – rich and thick with pearl barley and lean beef gobbets and golden carrot rings and fat little dumplings – so solidly good that it was said that a spoon would stand in it upright. For the sick there were custard puddings, home-made jellies and half-bottles of port, and it was an unwritten law in the parish that, by sending a plate to the vicarage at precisely 1.30 on any Sunday, a convalescent could claim a dinner from the vicarage joint. There were blankets at Christmas, unbleached calico chemises for girls on first going out in service, flannel petticoats for old women, and flannel-lined waistcoats for old men.

So it had been for a quarter of a century, and Mr and Mrs Coulsdon and their fat coachman, Thomas, and Hannah, the parlourmaid who doctored the villagers' lesser ailments with herb tea and ointments, and Gantry, the cook, and the spotted Dalmatian dog which ran behind Mrs Coulsdon's carriage, and the heavy carved mahogany furniture and rich damask hangings of the vicarage seemed to the villagers almost as firmly established and enduring as the church tower.

Then, one summer afternoon, Mrs Coulsdon, dressed in her best, drove off in her carriage to attend a large and fashionable bazaar and sale of work got up by the country notabilities, and, in addition to her many purchases, brought back with her the germ which killed her within a week. Her husband caught the infection and followed her a few days later and they were buried in one grave, to which their coffins were followed by the entire population of the parish, and sincerely mourned, for that one day at least, even by those who had scarcely given them a thought before. The *Candleford News* had a three-column account of the funeral, headed: 'The Candleford

Green Tragedy, Funeral of Beloved Vicar and His Wife', and the grave and the surrounding sward, covered with wreaths and crosses and pathetic little bunches of cottage-garden flowers, was photographed and copies were sold at fourpence each and framed and hung upon cottage walls.

Then the parishioners began to wonder what the new Vicar would be like. 'We shall be lucky if we get another as good as Mr Coulsdon,' they said. 'He was a gentleman as was a gentleman, and she was a lady. Never interfered with anybody's business, he didn't, and was good to the poor'; and 'Dealt with the local shops and paid on the nail,' added the shopkeepers.

Months later, after every room in the vicarage had been overhauled by workmen and the greater part of the garden and paddock had been torn up to get at the drains, which were naturally suspect, the new Vicar arrived, but he and his family belonged so much to the new order of things that they must be given a later place in this record.

It sometimes seems to us that some impression of those now dead must be left upon their familiar earthly surroundings. We saw them, on such a day, in such a spot, in such an attitude, smiling – or not smiling – and the impression of the scene is so deeply engraved upon our own hearts that we feel they must have left some more enduring trace, though invisible to mortal eyes. Or perhaps it would be better to say at present invisible, for the discovery of sound waves has opened up endless possibilities.

If any such impressions of good old Mr Coulsdon remain, one may be of him as Laura once saw him, brought to a halt on one of his daily progresses round the green. He stood, well-fed and well-groomed, in a world that seemed made for him, gravely shaking his head at a distant view of the gambols of the village idiot, as if asking himself the frequent question of lesser mortals, 'Why? Why?'

For Candleford Green had its village idiot in the form of a young man who had been born a deaf mute. At birth he was probably not mentally deficient, but he had been born too early to profit by the marvellous modern system of training such unfortunates, and had, as a child, been allowed to run wild while other children were in school, and the isolation and the absence of all means of communicating with his fellows had told upon him.

At the time when Laura knew him, he was a full-grown man, powerfully built, with a small golden beard his mother kept clipped and, in his quieter moments, an innocent rather than a vacant expression. His mother, who was a widow, took in washing, and he would fetch and carry her clothes-baskets, draw water from the well, and turn the handle of the mangle. At home the two of them used a rough language of signs which his mother had invented, but with the outside world he had no means of communication and, for that reason, coupled with that of his occasional fits of temper, although he was strong and probably capable of learning to do any simple manual work, no one would give him employment. He was known as Luney Joe.

Joe spent his spare time, which was the greater part of each day, lounging about the green, watching the men at work at the forge or in the carpenter's shop. Sometimes, after watching quietly for some time, he would burst into loud, inarticulate cries which were taken for laughter, then turn and run quickly out into the country, where he had many lairs in the woods and hedgerows. Then the men would laugh and say: 'Old Luney Joe's like the monkeys. They could talk if they'd a mind to, but they think if they did we'd set 'em to work.'

If he got in the way of the workmen, they would take him by the shoulders and run him outside, and it was chiefly his wild gestures, contortions of feature, and loud inarticulate cries at such times which had earned him his name.

'Luney Joe! Luney Joe!' the children would call out after him, secure in the knowledge that, whatever they said, he could not hear them. But, although he was deaf and dumb, Joe was not blind, and, once or twice, when he had happened to look round and see them following and mocking him, he had threatened them by shaking the ash stick he carried. The story of this lost nothing in the telling, and people were soon saying that Joe was getting dangerous and ought to be put away. But his mother fought stoutly for his liberty, and the doctor supported her. Joseph was sane enough, he said; his seeming strangeness came from his affliction. Those against him would do well to see that their own children were better behaved.

What went on in Joe's mind nobody knew, though his mother, who loved him, may have had some idea. Laura many times saw him standing to gaze on the green with knitted brows, as though puzzling as to why other young men should be batting and bowling there and himself left out. Once some men unloading logs to add to Miss Lane's winter store allowed Joe to hand down from the cart some of the heaviest, and, for a time, his face wore an expression of perfect happiness. After a while, unfortunately, his spirits soared and he began flinging the logs down wildly and, as a result, hit one of the men on the shoulder, and was turned away roughly. At that, he fell into one of his passions and, afterwards, people said that Luney Joe was madder than ever.

But he could be very gentle. Once Laura met him in a lonely spot between trees and she felt afraid, for the path was narrow and she was alone. But she felt ashamed of her cowardice afterwards, for, as she passed him, so closely that their elbows touched, the big fellow, gentle as a lamb, put out his hand and stroked some flowers she was carrying. With nods and smiles, Laura passed on, rather hurriedly, it must be confessed, but wishing more than ever she could do something to help him.

Some years after Laura had left the district she was told that, after his mother's death, Luney Joe had been sent to the County Asylum. Poor Joe! the world which went very well for some people in those days was a harsh one for the poor and afflicted. For the old and poor, too. That was long before the day of the Old Age Pension, and for many who had worked hard all their lives and had preserved their self-respect, so far, the only refuge in old age was the Work-house. There old couples were separated, the men going to the men's side and the women to that of the women, and the effect of this separation on some faithful old hearts can be imagined. With the help of a few shillings a week, parish relief, and the still fewer shillings their children – mostly poor like themselves – could spare, some old couples contrived to keep their own roof over their heads. Laura knew several such couples well. The old man, bent nearly double upon his stick, but clean and tidy, would appear at the Post Office periodically to cash some postal order for a tiny amount sent by a daughter in service or a married son. 'Thank God we've got good children,' he would say, with pride as well as gratitude in his tone, and Laura would answer: 'Yes, isn't Katie' – or Jimmy – 'splendid!'

In those days, if any one in a village was ill, it was the custom for neighbours to send them little dainties. Even Laura's mother, out of her poverty, would send a little of anything she thought a sick neighbour might fancy. Miss Lane, who had ten times the resources of Laura's mother, did things in style. In cases of sickness, as soon as she heard the patient had 'turned the corner', she would kill or buy and have cooked a fowl in order to send a dinner, and Laura, being the quickest walker, was deputed to carry the covered plate across the green. It was an act of kindness which blessed giver and receiver alike, for the best cut from the breast of the bird was always reserved for Miss Lane's own dinner. But perhaps that was not a bad plan; anticipation of the enjoyment of her own tit-bit may have acted as a stimulus to her good intention, and the invalids got the next-best cuts and broth was made from the bones for them later.

Zillah could be trusted to cook the chicken, but, once, when one of Miss Lane's own friends fell ill, she herself brought out from somewhere a cooking apron of fine white linen and, with her own hands, made him a wine jelly. The history of that jelly was far removed from that of those we now buy in bottles from the grocer. To begin upon, calf's feet were procured and simmered for the better part of a day to extract the nourishment.

Then the contents of the stewpan were strained and the stock had another long boiling in order to render it down to the desired strength and quantity. Then more straining and sweetening and lacing with port, sufficient to colour it a deep ruby, and clearing with eggshells, and straining and straining. Then it was poured into a flannel jellybag, the shape of a fool's cap, which had to hang from a hook in the larder ceiling all night to let its contents ooze through into the vessel placed beneath, without squeezing, and when, at last, all the complicated processes were completed, it was poured into a small mould and allowed yet one more night in which to set. No gelatine was used.

What Miss Lane called 'a taster' was reserved for herself in a teacup, and of this she gave Laura and Zillah a teaspoonful each that they might also taste. To Laura's untutored palate, it tasted no better than the red jujube sweets of which she was fond, but Zillah, out of her greater experience, declared that a jelly so strong and delicious would 'a'most raise the dead'.

Few would care to take that trouble for the sake of a few spoonfuls of jelly in these days. Laura's aunts delighted in such cookery and her mother would have enjoyed doing it had her means permitted, but already it was thought a waste of time in many households. On the face of it, it does seem absurd to spend the inside of a week making a small jelly, and women were soon to have other uses for their time and energy, but those who did such cookery in those days looked upon it as an art, and no time or trouble was thought wasted if the result were perfection. We may call the Victorian woman ignorant, weak, clinging and vapourish – she is not here to answer such charges – but at least we must admit that she knew how to cook.

Another cooking process Laura was never to see elsewhere and which perhaps may have been peculiar to smithy families was known as 'salamandering'. For this thin slices of bacon or ham were spread out on a large plate and taken to the smithy, where the plate was placed on the anvil. The smith then heated red-hot one end of a large, flat iron utensil known as the 'salamander' and held it above the plate until the rashes were crisp and curled. Shelled boiled, or poached, eggs were eaten with this dish.

Bath nights at Candleford Green were conducted on the old country system. There was near the back door an old out-building formerly used as a brew-house. Miss Lane could remember when all the beer for the house and the smiths was brewed there. In Laura's time it came from the brewery in nine-gallon casks. The custom of home brewing was fading out in farmers' and tradesmen's households; it saved trouble and expense to buy the beer from the brewery in barrels; but a few belonging to the older generation still brewed at home for themselves and their workmen. At the Candleford Green Post Office Laura issued about half a dozen four-shilling home-brewing licences a year. One woman there kept an off-licence and brewed her own beer. There was a large old yew tree at the bottom of her garden, and her customers sat beneath its spreading branches on the green, just outside her garden wall, and consumed their drinks 'off the premises' in compliance with the law. But, as she brewed for sale, hers must have been a more expensive licence, probably issued by the magistrates.

Miss Lane's brew-house had become a bath-house. It was not used by Miss Lane or by Zillah. Miss Lane took what she called her 'canary dip' in a large, shallow, saucer-shaped bath in her bedroom in a few inches of warm rain water well laced with *eau de cologne*. In winter she had a bedroom fire on her weekly bath night, and in all seasons the bath was protected by a screen – not, as might be supposed, to preserve Victorian modesty, but to keep off draughts. On the farm churning days a quart of buttermilk was delivered for Miss Lane's toilet. That was for her face and hands. When, where, and how Zillah bathed was a mystery. When baths in general were mentioned, she said she hoped she knew how to keep herself clean without boiling herself like a pig's cheek. As she always appeared very fresh and clean, Laura supposed she must have bathed by the old cottage method of washing all over in a basin. The smiths, on account of the grubby, black nature of their work, needed baths frequently, and for them, in the first place, the brew-house had been turned into a bathroom. Wednesdays and Saturdays were their bath nights. Laura's was Friday.

In one corner of the bath-house stood the old brewing copper, now connected by a length of hose-pipe, passing through the window, with the pump in the yard for filling purposes. A tap a few feet above floor level served to draw off the water when hot. On the brick floor stood the deep, man-length zinc bath used by the smiths, and standing up-ended in a corner when not in use was the hip bath for Laura and for any visitor to the house who preferred, as they said, 'a good hot soak to sitting in a saucer'. There was a square of matting rolled up, ready to be put down by the bather, and a curtain at the window and another over the door to keep out prying eyes and cold air.

To Laura the brew-house baths seemed luxurious. She had been used to bathing at home in the wash-house in water heated over the fire in a cauldron, but there every drop of water had to be fetched from a well and, fuel being equally precious, the share of hot water for each person was small. 'A good scrub all over and a rinse and make way for the next' were her mother's instructions. At Candleford Green there was unlimited hot water – boiling water which filled the small building with steam, for the fire beneath it had been lighted by the smithy apprentice before he left work, and by eight o'clock the water in the copper was bubbling. With curtains drawn over window and door and red embers glowing beneath the copper, Laura would sit, with her knees drawn up, in hot water up to her neck and luxuriate.

She was often to think of those baths in later years when she stepped into or out of the few inches of tepid water in her clean but cold modern bathroom or looked at the geyser, ticking the pennies away, and wondered if it would be too extravagant to let it run longer. But perhaps the unlimited hot water did less to make the brew-house baths memorable than the youth, health, and freedom from care of the bather.

The community was largely self-supporting. Every household grew its own vegetables, produced its new-laid eggs and cured its own bacon. Jams and jellies, wines and pickles, were made at home as a matter of course. Most gardens had a row of beehives. In the houses of the well-to-do there was an abundance of such foods, and even the poor enjoyed a rough plenty. The problem facing the lower-paid workers was not so much how to provide food for themselves and their families as how to obtain the hundred and one other things, such as clothing, boots, fuel, bedding and crockery ware, which had to be paid for in cash.

Those with an income of ten or twelve shillings a week often had to go short of such things, although the management and ingenuity of some of the women was amazing. Every morsel of old rag they could save or beg was made into rugs for the stone floors, or cut into fragments to make flocks to stuff bedding. Sheets were turned outside into middle and, after they had again become worn, patched and patched again until it was difficult to decide which part of a sheet was the original fabric. 'Keep the flag flying!' they would call to each other when they had their Monday morning washing flapping on the line, and the seeing eye and the feeling heart, had the possessor of these been present, would have read more than was meant into the saying. They kept the flag flying nobly, but the cost to themselves was great.

IV

Penny Reading

In those days, when young or progressive inhabitants of Candleford Green complained of the dullness of village life, the more staid would say, 'It may be dull in some villages; but not here. Why, there's always something going on!' which the dissatisfied could not deny, for, although there was none of the amusement they desired, amusements of a kind were plentiful.

No films, of course, for twenty years had yet to pass before Candleford town had its Happidrome, and no dancing for the ordinary villager except dancing on the green at holiday times in summer. But there were in winter the Church Social, with light refreshments and indoor games, and monthly Penny Readings, and a yearly concert in the schoolroom. Between these highlights of the social year, there were sewing parties which met at each of the members' houses in turn, when one of the members read aloud while the others sewed garments for the heathen or for the poor in cities, and tea was provided by the hostess of the occasion. The work parties were for the better-to-do. The cottagers had their Mothers' Meetings, which were very similar, except that there the members sewed for themselves and their families materials provided at under cost price by the ladies of the Committee, and there was no tea.

The reading aloud must have made slow progress, judging by the amount of talking done at both types of sewing party. The repetition of every spicy item of village gossip was prefaced by: 'Mrs So-and-So was saying at the working party –' Or: 'I heard somebody say at the Mothers' Meeting –' The fact was that both were clearing-houses for gossip, but that did not make them less enjoyable.

In summer there were 'the outings'. That of the Mothers' Meeting, after weeks of discussion of more or less desirable seaside resorts, always decided for London and the Zoo. The Choir Outing left in the small hours of the morning for Bournemouth or Weston-super-Mare; and the Children's School Treat Outing went, waving flags and singing, in a horse wagonette to the vicarage paddock in a neighbouring village, where tea and buns were partaken of at a long trestle table under some trees. After tea they ran races and played games, and returned home, tired and grubby, but still noisy, to find even a larger crowd than had seen them off waiting on the green to welcome them and join in their 'Hip-hip-hooray!'

The Penny Reading was a form of entertainment already out of date in most places; but at Candleford Green it was still going strong in the 'nineties. For it the schoolroom was lent, free of charge, 'By kind permission of the Managers', as stated upon the handbills, and the pennies taken at the door paid for heating and light. It was a popular as well as an inexpensive entertainment. Everybody went; whole families together, and all agreed that the excitement of going out after dark, carrying lanterns, and sitting in a warm room with rows and rows of other people, was well worth the sum of one penny, apart from the entertainment provided.

The star turn was given by an old gentleman from a neighbouring village, who, in his youth, had heard Dickens read his own works in public and aimed at reproducing in his own rendering the expression and mannerisms of the master.

Old Mr Greenwood put a tremendous amount of nervous energy into his reading. His features expressed as much as his voice, and his free hand was never still, and if the falsetto of his female characters sometimes rose to a screech, his facetious young men were almost too slyly humorous, and some of his listeners felt embarrassed when the deep, low voice he kept for pathetic passages broke and he had to pause to wipe away real tears, his rendering still had an authentic ring which to Dickens lovers was, as the villagers said about other items, 'well worth listening to'.

The bulk of his audience did not criticize; it enjoyed. The comic passages, featuring Pickwick, Dick Swiveller, or Sairy Gamp, were punctuated with bursts of laughter. Oliver Twist asking for more and the deathbed of Little Nell drew tears from the women and throat-clearings from the men. The reader was so regularly encored that he had been obliged to cut down his items on the programme to two; which, in effect, was four, and, when he had finished his last reading and, with his hand on his heart, had bowed himself from the platform, people would sigh and say to each other: 'Whatever comes next'll sound dull after that!'

They showed so much interest that one would naturally have expected them to get Dickens's books, of which there were several in the Parish Library, to read for themselves. But, with a very few exceptions, they did not, for, although they liked to listen, they were not readers. They were waiting, a public ready-made, for the wireless and the cinema.

Another penny reader whose items Laura enjoyed was a Mrs Cox, who lived in the Dower House on one of the neighbouring estates and was said to be an American by birth. She was middle-aged, dressed unconventionally in loose, collarless frocks, usually green, and had short iron-grey hair which hung loose in curls, like a modern bob. She always read from *Uncle Remus*, and her rendering of Brer Rabbit and Brer Fox and the tar-baby may have owed something to some old black mammy of her childhood. The rich huskiness of her tone, her plantation dialect, and her flashing smile when delivering some side-thrust of wit were charming.

For the rest, some of the readings were well chosen, some ill chosen. A few poems were interspersed between the prose passages, but these seldom rose higher than 'Excelsior', or 'The Village Blacksmith', or 'The Wreck of the Hesperus'. Once Laura had the honour of choosing two passages for the father of one of her friends, who had been invited to read and could not, as he said, think of anything likely, not if his life depended upon it. She chose the scene from *The Heart of Midlothian* in which Jeanie Deans is granted an audience by Queen Caroline and the chapter about the Battle of Waterloo from *Vanity Fair* which ends: 'Darkness came down on the field and city; and Amelia was praying for George, who was lying on his face, dead, with a bullet through his heart.' The man who read them said he thought they went down very well with the audience, but Laura did not notice any marked interest.

For the homely Penny Reading, second-best wear was considered sufficient; that being the last outfit before the newest, which, sponged and pressed and smartened up by the addition of a new ribbon bow and lace collar, had to serve another term for better wear before being taken into everyday use. At the annual concert the audience appeared in churchgoing Sunday best. The young ladies contributing to the programme wore white or pale-coloured frocks with a modest 'v' neck and elbow sleeves, and the village girls who appeared on the platform their last summer's frock with a flower in their hair, or an ivy wreath, or a bright ribbon bow. For the Church Social, summer frocks were worn by the girls – last year's in most cases, but, in a few, next year's made in advance and worn with the collar tucked in to give it an evening-dress appearance. The older women wore black silk if they had it; if not, the stiffest and richest fabric they possessed or could afford to buy for the occasion.

The fashion in dress was by that time more simple than it had been. The bustle had long passed away, and with it had gone panniers, waterfall backs, and other drapings on skirts. The new plain skirt was long and full and slightly stiffened at the hem to make it stand out well round the ankles, and, with it went a blouse or bodice, as the upper part of a frock was still called, with balloon sleeves and a full, loose front, often of a contrasting colour. Small waists were still fashionable, but the standard of smallness had changed. Women no longer aimed at an eighteen- or twenty-inch span, but were satisfied with one of twenty-two, -three, or -four inches, and that had to be attained by moderate compression; the old savage tight-lacing was a thing of the past.

In hairdressing, the Royal, or Alexandra, fringe was the rage. For this the hair was cut above the forehead and curled, or, rather, frizzed to reach back almost to the crown. Considering that this style of hairdressing was introduced by the then Princess of Wales whose beauty and goodness and taste as a leader of fashion was unchallenged, it is strange that it should have been condemned by many as 'fast'. As in the case of bobbing during the last war, men and older women objected extravagantly to the fringe; but they had to get used to it, for, like the bob, it was a becoming fashion and it had come to stay. Fringes were worn all through the 'nineties.

Laura, dressing for the Church Social in the cream nun's veiling frock in which she had been confirmed and in which her cousins Molly and Nellie had been confirmed before her, wondered if she might venture to cut and curl a few locks on her own forehead. If Miss Lane or her mother noticed them and objected, she could say they were little loose ends she had curled up to make them tidier, or, if they passed unnoticed, she could cut and curl more, and so get a fringe by instalments. The stem of a new clay pipe borrowed from Matthew's bedroom served her as a substitute for curling-tongs when heated in the flame of her candle, and she pushed her hat low down on her brow before going downstairs. There were comments and some criticism afterwards. Her brother told her she looked like a young prize bull, and her mother said, 'It suits you, of course, but you're too young to go thinking of fashions.' But, by degrees, she got her fringe, and a troublesome job it was to keep it in curl in wet weather.

The Church Social was strictly a villagers' affair. No one came from the great houses and the clergyman only looked in once during the evening. The presence of the curate and Sunday-School teachers guaranteed propriety. When the mothers had assisted with clearing away the tea and the long trestle tables had been removed, they seated themselves around the walls to watch the games. After 'Postman's Knock' and 'Musical Chairs' and 'Here we go round the Mulberry Bush', a large ring was formed for 'Dropping the Handkerchief' and the fun of the evening began. '*I wrote a letter to my love and on the way I dropped it. One of you has picked it up and put it in your pocket,*' chanted the odd man or girl out as they circled the ring, handkerchief in hand, until they came to the back of the person they wished to choose and placed the handkerchief on his or her shoulder. The chase which followed took so long, round and round the ring and always eventually out of one of the several doors, that two separate handkerchiefs kept two couples going in the Church

Social version of the game. There was supposed to be no kissing, as it was a Church function, but when the pursuer caught the pursued somewhere beyond the door with a smudged roller towel upon it, who could say what happened. Perhaps the youth sketched a stage kiss. Perhaps not.

As the evening went on, the women and girls and young men and boys in the ring whirled hand in hand, faster and faster, the girls' blue and pink and green skirts standing out like bells and the young men's faces getting redder, until some one called out, 'Time for "Auld Lang Syne"!' and hands were crossed and the old song was sung and people went home, in families or couples, according to age. Dancing would have been better perhaps, but 'Dropping the Handkerchief' served much the same purpose in that unsophisticated day.

From such festivities some of the older girls were seen home by young men. The engaged, of course, were already provided with an escort, and for that office to certain unattached pretty and popular girls there was keen rivalry. The young and not in any way outstanding girls, such as Laura, had to find their way home through the darkness alone, or join up with some family or group of friends which happened to be going their way.

One year and one year only at the Church Social, after the singing of 'Auld Lang Syne', a young man approached Laura and said, bowing gravely as was the custom, 'May I have the pleasure of seeing you home?' This caused quite a sensation among those immediately surrounding the pair, for the young man was the reporter for the local newspaper and so looked upon as an outsider at such gatherings. His predecessor had sat about with a bored air between his dashes out to the 'Golden Lion', and once, when invited to join hands in the final singing, had refused and stood aloof in a corner scribbling in his note-book. But he was a middle-aged man and inclined to give himself airs. This new reporter, who had appeared for the first time at Candleford Green that evening, was only a year or two older than Laura, and he had joined in the games and laughed and shouted as loudly as anybody. He had nice blue eyes and an infectious laugh, and, of course, the note-book in which he scribbled shorthand notes was also attractive to Laura. So, when he asked her if he might see her home, she was delighted to murmur the conventional 'That would be very kind of you'.

As they circled the green in the mild, damp air of the winter night, he told Laura about himself. He had only left school a few months before and was being given a month's trial by the Editor of the *Candleford News*. The month of trial was almost over and he would be leaving Candleford in a day or two, not because he had proved unsatisfactory – at least he hoped not – but because a much better opening had now been found for him by his parents on a newspaper in his home town, far up in the midlands. 'After that, Fleet Street, I suppose?' suggested Laura, and they both laughed at that as an excellent joke and agreed that they both felt they must have met before at sometime, somewhere. Then they had to discuss the party they had come from and to laugh at some of the oddities there. Which was wrong of Laura, who had been carefully trained never to make fun of the absent. The only excuse that can be found for her is that it was the first time she met any one from the outside world near her own age and upon anything like equal terms, and that may have gone to her head a little.

They laughed and chattered until they came to the Post Office door; then stood talking in hushed voices until their feet grew cold and her companion suggested that they should take another turn round the green to restore their circulation. They took several turns, for they began talking about books and forgot how late it was growing, and they might, indeed, have continued walking and talking all night had not a light appeared at the Post Office door, when Laura, after a hasty 'Good night', hurried there to find Miss Lane looking out for her.

Laura never saw Godfrey Parrish again, but for some years they wrote to each other. His were amusing letters, written on the best editorial notepaper, thick and good, with a black embossed heading. As his letters often ran to seven or eight pages, his editor must sometimes have marvelled at the rapidity with which his private stock of notepaper became depleted. In return, Laura told him of any amusing little incident which occurred and what books she was reading, until, at last, the correspondence languished, then ceased, in the usual manner of such pen-friendships.

Beyond having a friend or relative to stay with her occasionally, Miss Lane did little entertaining. She said she saw as much of her neighbours as she desired at the Post Office counter. But once a year she gave what she called her 'hay-home supper', and that to those of her household was a great occasion.

She had two small paddocks beyond her garden in one or other of which Peggy, the old chestnut mare, took her ease when her services were not required to draw the smiths with their tools in the spring-cart to the hunting stables. Every spring one of the paddocks was shut up for hay. Its yield was one small haystack, a quantity quite out of proportion to the bustle and excitement of the hay-home supper, but the making of hay for the pony's winter fodder and the supper for all those who had worked for her in any capacity during the year was part of the traditional business and domestic economy handed down to Miss Lane by her parents and grandparents. Excepting Laura, the younger smiths, and Miss Lane herself, who was ageless, all at the hay-home supper were elderly or old. There were grey and white heads all around the table and the custom itself was so hoary that that must have been one of its last manifestations.

For the haymaking a queer old couple named Beer were engaged, not for the day, week, or season, but permanently. On some fine summer morning, without previous notice, Beer would come with his scythe to the back door and say: 'Tell Mis'is that grass be in fine fettle now an' th' weather don't look too unkind like; and with her permission I be now about to begin on't.' When he had the grass lying in swathes, his wife appeared, and together they raked and turned and tossed and tedded, refreshed at short intervals by jugs of beer or tea provided by Miss Lane and carried to them by Zillah.

Beer was a typical old countryman, ruddy and wizened, with very bright eyes; shrivelled and thin of figure and sagging at the knees, but still sprightly. His wife was also ruddy of face, but her figure was as round as a barrel. Instead of the usual sun bonnet, she wore for the haymaking a white muslin frilled cap tied under the chin, and over it a broad-brimmed black straw hat, which made her look like an old-fashioned Welsh-woman. She was a merry old soul with a fat, chuckling laugh, and when she laughed her face wrinkled up until her eyes disappeared. She was much in request as a midwife.

When the hay was dried and in cocks, Beer came to the door again: 'Ma'am, ma'am!' he would call. 'We be ready.' That was the signal for the smiths to turn out and build the hayrick, with Peggy herself and her spring-cart to do the carrying. All that day there was much running to and fro and shouting and merriment. Indoors, the kitchen table was laid with pies and tarts and custards and, in the place of honour at the head of the table, the dish of the evening, a stuffed collar chine of bacon. When the company assembled, large, foaming jugs of beer would be drawn for the men and for those of the women who preferred it. A jug of home-made lemonade with a sprig of borage floating at the top circulated at the upper end of the table.

For the stuffed chine the largest dish in the house had to be used. It was a great round joint, being the whole neck of a pig, cut and cured specially for the hay-home supper. It was lavishly stuffed with sage and onions and was altogether very rich and highly flavoured. It would not have suited modern digestions, but most of those present at the hay-home supper ate of it largely and enjoyed it. Old Mr Beer, in the little speech he made after supper, never forgot to mention the chine. 'I've been a-meakin' hay in them fields f'r this forty-six 'ears,' he would say, 'in your time, ma'am, an' y'r feyther's an' y'r gran'fer's before yer, an' th' stuffed chines I've a-eaten at the suppers've always bin of the best; but of all the chines I've tasted in this kitchen that of which I sees the remains before me – if remains they can be called, f'r you wants to put on y'r spectacles to see 'em – wer' the finest an' fattest an' teastiest of any.'

After Miss Lane had replied to the speech of thanks, home-made wine was brought out, tobacco and snuff handed round, and songs were sung. It was a point of strict etiquette that every guest should contribute something to the programme, irrespective of musical ability. The songs were sung without musical accompaniment and many of them without a recognizable tune, but what they may have lacked in harmony was more than made up for in length.

Every year when Laura was present Mr Beer obliged with his famous half-song, half-recitation, relating the adventures of an Oxfordshire man on a trip to London. It began:

> Last Michaelmas I remember well, when harvest wer' all over,
> Our chaps had stacked up all the be-ans and re-aked up all th'
>   clover,

which lull in the year's work gave one Sam the daring idea of taking a trip to Town:

> For Sal went there a year ago, along wi' Squire Brown,
> Housemaid or summat, doan't know what,
> To live in Lunnon town,
> An' they behaved right well to Sal an' give her cloathes an' that,
> An' Sal 'aved nation well to them and got quite tall and fat.

So Sam thought, if 'Measter' approved, he would pay his sister a visit. 'If "Measter" refused permission', Sam said in quite a modern spirit:

> Old Grograin then must give I work, a rum old fellow he!
> He grumbles when he sets us on, but, dang it! what care we.

But he had still his mother to deal with. She 'cried aloud to break her heart at parting thus with me'; but cheered up and began to look into ways and means:

> Well, since you 'ull so headstrong be, some rigging we must get,
> I'll wash 'ee out another shirt, an' sprig 'ee up a bit,

and gave as her parting advice:

> Now, Sam, 'ave well where you be gwain,
> Whatever others does to you, be sure don't turn again.

To which Sam replied:

> Yes, very purty, fancy that now, blow me jacket tight!
> If they begins their rigs wi' me, I'll purty soon show fight,

and cut himself a good stout ash stick before setting out in his 'holland smock, as good as new' on foot to 'Lunnon town'.

To her children's disgust in after years, Laura's memory left him, newly arrived, on London Bridge, asking passers-by if they knew 'our Sal, or mayhap Squire Brown', but there were stanzas and stanzas after that – that one song, in fact, accounted for a good part of the evening. But no one then present found it too long, for the younger smiths had slipped, one by one, out of the door, and those left, excepting Laura and Miss Lane, were old and loved the old, slow, country manner of rejoicing.

They sat around the table. Mrs Beer with her arms folded on her comfortable stomach and one ear always open to catch what she called 'a bidding', for 'My dear, 'tis a mortal truth that babbies like to come arter dark. For why? So's nobody should see their blessed little spirits come winging'; Beer himself beaming on all and inclined to hiccups towards the end of the evening; the old washerwoman's worn fingers fingering her muslin cap, only worn on special occasions; Zillah, important and fussy, acting the part of a second hostess; and Matthew, with his old blue eyes shining with gratification at the laughter which greeted his jokes. Miss Lane, very upright at the head of the table in her claret-coloured silk, looked like a visitant from another sphere, well weighted down to earth, though, by her gold chains and watch and brooches and locket; and Laura, in pink print, ran in and out with plates and glasses, because it was Zillah's evening off. That was the hay-home supper, a survival, though perhaps not more ancient than a couple of hundred years or so – a mere babe of a survival compared to the Village Feast.

The maypole had long been chopped up for firewood, the morris dance was fading out as one after another the old players died, and Plough Monday had become an ordinary working day; but at Candleford Green the Feast was still a general holiday, as it must have been from the day upon which the church was dedicated, far back in the centuries.

Some kind of feast may have been held on the green before that time, some pagan rite, for even in the respectable latter part of the nineteenth century there was more of a pagan than a Christian spirit abroad at the Feast celebrations.

It was essentially a people's holiday. The clergy and the local gentle-people had no hand in it. They avoided the green on that day. Even the youngest of country house-parties had not yet discovered the delights of hurdy-gurdy music and naphtha flares, of shouting oneself hoarse in swingboats and waving paper streamers while riding mechanical ostriches. With one exception to be mentioned hereafter, only a few of the under-servants from the great houses appeared on the green on Feast Monday.

For those who liked feasts there were booths and stalls and coconut shies and shooting-galleries and swingboats and a merry-go-round and a brass band for dancing. All the fun of the fair, in fact. From early morning people poured in from the neighbouring villages and from Candleford town.

Candleford Green people were proud of this display. It showed how the place had come on, they said, for the largest and most brilliantly painted and lit merry-go-round in the county to find it worth while to attend their Feast. Old men could remember when there had been only one booth with a two-headed calf or a fat lady, and a few poor stalls selling ginger bread or the pottery images still to be seen in some of their cottages, representing a couple in bed in nightcaps, and the bedroom utensil showing beneath the bed-valance.

In those early days there had been no merry-go-round, but for the children, they said, there was Old Hickman's whirligig, apparently the parent of the modern merry-go-round. It was made entirely of wood, with an outside circle of plain wooden seats which revolved by means of a hand-turned device in the centre. It was a one-man show. When Old Hickman grew tired, a boy bystander was invited to take his place at the handle, the promised reward being a ride for every twenty minutes' labour. While the old men were still boys, this primitive merry-go-round collapsed and they made a rhyme about it, which ran:

> Old Jim Hickman's whirligig broke down,
> Broke and let the wenches down.
> If that'd been made of ash or oak,
> I'll be blowed if that'd have broke.

Old Hickman's whirligig had broken down and gone to the bonfire fifty years before, and only Laura cared to hear about it. That, she was told, was because she was 'one of the quiet, old-fashioned sort'. But 'still waters run deep', they would remind her, and there were plenty of sweethearts to go round and suit all.

There were plenty of sweethearts on the green on Feast Monday, pairs and pairs and pairs of them, the girls in their best summer frocks, with flowers or feathers in their hats, and the young men in their Sunday suits, with pink or blue ties. With arms round each other's waists, they strolled from one sight to the next, eating sweets or sections of coconut; or took turns on the merry-go-round or in the swingboats. All day the roundabout organ ground out its repertoire of popular tunes, in competition with the brass band playing a different tune at the other end of the green. Swingboats appeared and disappeared over the canvas roofs of the booths, and the occupants, now head upwards, now feet upwards, shrieked with excitement and cheered each other on to go higher and still higher, while, below, on the trampled turf, people of all ages threaded the narrow passages between the shows, laughing and shouting and eating – always eating.

'What crowds!' people cried. 'It's the best Feast we've ever had. If the green could only always look like this! And I do dearly love a bit of good music.'

The noise was deafening. The few quiet people who stayed indoors put cotton-wool in their ears. One year when a poor woman was dying on Feast Monday in a cottage near the green her friends went out and begged that the band would stop playing for an hour. The band, of course, could not stop playing but the bandsmen offered to muffle the drumsticks, and, for the rest of the afternoon the drum's *dum, dum, dum* sounded a *memento mori* amidst the rejoicings. Very few noticed it, the other noises were too many and too loud, and by teatime its resonance was restored, for the woman had died.

Every year, among the cottagers and show folk and maidservants and farm-hands at the Feast, there was one aristocratic figure. It was that of a young man, the eldest son of a peer, who for years frequented all the feasts and fairs and club-walkings of the countryside. Laura knew him well by sight, for his ancestral mansion was not far from her own home. From her window at Candleford Green Post Office she once saw him, leaning languidly against the pay-box of a coconut shy, surrounded by a bevy of girls who were having 'tries' at the coconuts at his expense. His dress was that of a country gentleman of his time, tweed Norfolk suit and deerstalker cap, and that, and his air of ironic detachment, set him apart from the crowd and helped out his Childe Harold pose.

All day he was surrounded by village girls, waiting to be treated to the different shows, and from these he would select one favourite with whom to dance the evening through. His group was a centre of interest. 'Have 'ee seen Lord So-and-So?' people would ask, just as they might have asked, 'Have 'ee seen the fat lady?' or 'the peep-show?' and they openly pointed him out to each other as one of the sights of the Feast.

The heroine of a modern novel would have seized such an opportunity to go out into the throng and learn a little at first-hand about life; but this is a true story, and Laura was not of the stuff of which heroines are made. A born looker-on, she preferred to watch from her window, excepting one year when her brother Edmund came and took her out and knocked off so many coconuts from the 'shy' that its proprietor refused his penny for another go, saying in aggrieved tones: 'I know your sort. You bin practising.'

Early in the evening the merry-go-round packed up and departed. It had only stopped there to put in a day on its way to a larger and more remunerative fair in the locality. After its organ had gone, the strains of the band music could be heard and the number of dancers increased. Shop girls and their swains arrived from Candleford town, farm workers from outlying villages came, arm in arm with their girls; men- and maidservants from the great houses stole out for an hour, and an occasional passer-by, attracted by the sounds of revelry, came forward and found a partner.

Stalls and booths were taken down and their owners departed; tired family parties trailed home through the dust and unattached men retired to the public-houses, but for many there the fun was only beginning. The music went on and the pale summer frocks of the girl dancers glimmered on in the twilight.

V

Neighbours

In the early 'nineties the change which had for some time been going on in the outer world had reached Candleford Green. A few old-fashioned country homes, such as that of Miss Lane, might still be seen there, especially among those of the farming class, and long-established family businesses still existed, side by side with those newly established or brought up to date; but, as the older householders died and the proprietors of the old-fashioned businesses died or retired, the old gave place to the new.

Tastes and ideas were changing. Quality was less in demand than it had been. The old solid, hand-made productions, into which good materials and many hours of patient skilled craftsmanship had been put, were comparatively costly. The new machine-made goods cost less and had the further attraction of a meretricious smartness. Also they were fashionable, and most people preferred them on that account.

'Time, like an ever-rolling stream, bears all its sons away,' and its daughters, too, and the tastes and ideas of each generation, together with its ideals and conventions, go rolling downstream with it like so much debris. But, because the generations overlap, the change is gradual. In the country at the time now recorded, the day of the old skilled master-craftsman, though waning, was not over.

Across the green, almost opposite to the post office, stood a substantial cottage, end to end with a carpenters' shop. In most weathers the big double door of the workshop stood open and white-aproned workmen with their feet ankle-deep in shavings could be seen sawing and planing and shaping at the benches, with, behind them, a window framing a glimpse of a garden with old-fashioned flowers and a grape-vine draping a grey wall.

There lived and worked the three Williams, father, son, and grandson. With the help of a couple of journeymen, they not only did all the carpentry and joinery of the district at a time when no doors or mantelpieces or window-frames came ready made from abroad, but they also made and mended furniture for the use of the living and made coffins for the dead. There was no rival shop. The elder William was the carpenter of the village, just as Miss Lane was the postmistress and Mr Coulsdon the vicar.

Although less popular than the smithy as a gathering place, the carpenters' shop had also its habitués: older and graver men, as a rule, especially choirmen, for the eldest William played the organ in church and the middle William was choirmaster. Old Mr Stokes not only played the organ, but he had built it with his own hands, and these services to the Church and to music had given him a unique local standing. But he was almost as much valued for his great experience and his known wisdom. To him the villagers went in trouble or difficulty, and he was never known to fail them. He had been Miss Lane's father's close and intimate friend and was then her own.

At the time Laura knew him he was nearly eighty and much troubled by asthma, but he still worked at his trade occasionally, with his long, lean form swathed in a white apron and his full white beard buttoned into his waistcoat; and, on summer evenings, when the rolling peal of the organ came from the open door of the church, passers-by would say: 'That's old Mr Stokes playing, I'll lay! And he's playing his own music, too, I shouldn't wonder.' Sometimes he *was* playing his own music, for he would improvise for hours, but he loved more to play for his own pleasure the music of the masters.

The second William was unlike his father in appearance, being short and thick of figure while his father was as straight and almost as thin as a lath. His face resembled that of Dante Gabriel Rossetti so closely that Laura, on seeing the portrait of that poet-painter in later years, exclaimed, 'Mr William!' For, of course, he was called

'Mr William'. His father was always spoken of respectfully as 'Mr Stokes', and his nephew as 'Young Willie'.

Like his father, Mr William was both musician and craftsman of the old school, and it was naturally expected that as a matter of course these gifts would descend to the third William. It had been a proud day for old Mr Stokes when young Willie's indentures were signed, for he thought he saw in them an assured future for the old family business. When he was at rest, and his son, there would still be a William Stokes, Carpenter and Joiner, of Candleford Green, and, after that, perhaps, still another William to follow.

But Willie himself was not so sure. He had been legally apprenticed to his grandfather's business, as was the custom in family establishments in those days, rather because it was the line laid down for him than because he desired to become a carpenter. His work in the shop was to him but work, not a fine art or a religion, and for the music so sacred to his elders he had but a moderate taste.

He was a tall, slim boy of sixteen, with beautiful hazel eyes and a fair – too fair – pink-and-white complexion. Had his mother or his grandmother been alive, his alternating fits of lassitude and devil-may-care high spirits would have been recognized as a sign that he was outgrowing his strength and that his health needed care. But the only woman in his grandfather's house was a middle-aged cousin of the middle William, who acted as housekeeper: a hard, gaunt, sour-looking woman whose thoughts and energies were centred upon keeping the house spotless. When the front door of their house was opened upon the small bare hall, with its grandfather's clock and oil-cloth floor-covering patterned with lilies, an intruding nose was met by the clean, cold smell of soap and furniture polish. Everything in that house which could be scrubbed was scrubbed to a snowy whiteness; not a chair or a rug or a picture-frame was ever a hairbreadth out of place; horsehair chair and sofa coverings were polished to a cold slipperiness, table-tops might have served as mirrors, and an air of comfortless order pervaded the whole place. It was indeed a model house in the matter of cleanliness, but as a home for a delicate, warm-hearted orphan boy it fell short.

The kitchen was the only inhabited room. There the three generations of Williams took their meals, and there they carefully removed
their shoes before retiring to the bedrooms which were sleeping-
places only. To come home with wet clothes on a rainy day was
accounted a crime. The drying of them 'messed up the place', so
Willie, who was the only one of the three to be out in such weather,
would change surreptitiously and leave his clothes to dry as they
might, or not dry. His frequent colds left him with a cough that
lingered every year into the spring. 'A churchyard cough,' the older
villagers said, and shook their heads knowingly. But his grandfather
did not appear to notice this. Although he loved him tenderly, he
had too many other interests to be able to keep a close watch over
his grandson's physical well-being. He left that to the cousin, who
was absorbed in her housework and already felt it a hardship to
have what she called 'a great hulking hobble-de-hoy' in the house
to mess up her floors and rugs and made enough cooking and
washing up for a regiment.

Willie did not care for the music his grandfather and uncle loved.
He preferred the banjo and such popular songs as 'Oh, dem Golden
Slippers' and 'Two Lovely Black Eyes' to organ fugues – except in
church, where he sometimes sang the anthem, looking like an angel
in his white surplice.

Yet, in other ways, he had a great love of and craving for beauty.
'I do like deep, rich colours – violet and crimson and the blue of
these delphiniums – don't you?' he said to Laura in Miss Lane's
garden one day. Laura loved those colours, too. She was almost
ashamed to answer the questions in the Confession Books of her
more fashionable friends: *Favourite colours?* Purple and crimson.
Favourite flowers? The red rose. *Favourite poet?* Shakespeare. The
answers made her appear so unoriginal. She almost envied previous
writers in the books their preferences when she read: *Favourite
flower?* Petunia, orchid, or sweet-pea; but she had not as yet the
social wit to say, 'Favourite flower? After the rose, of course?' or to
pay mere lip service to Shakespeare, so she was obliged to appear
obvious.

Willie was fond of reading, too, and did not object to poetry.

Somehow he had got possession of an old shattered copy of an anthology called *A Thousand and One Gems* and when he came to tea with Miss Lane, who had known his mother and had a special affection for him, he would bring this book, and after office hours Laura and he would sit among the nut-trees at the bottom of the garden and take turns at reading aloud from it.

Those were the days for Laura when almost everything in literature was new to her and every fresh discovery was like one of Keats's own *Magic casements opening on the foam*. Between the shabby old covers of that one book were the 'Ode to a Nightingale', Shelley's 'Skylark', Wordsworth's 'Ode to Duty', and other gems which could move to a heart-shaking rapture. Willie took their readings more calmly. He liked where Laura loved. But he did honestly like, and that meant much to Laura, for none of those she had previously known in her short life, except her brother Edmund, cared twopence for poetry.

But one incident she shared with Willie remained more vivid in her memory than the poetry readings or the scrapes he got into with other boys, such as being let down into a well by the chain to rescue a duck which had spent a day and a night, quacking loudly, as it searched in vain for a shore to that deep, narrow pool into which it had tumbled, or the time when the hayrick was on fire and, against the advice of older men, he climbed to the top to beat the burning thatch with a rake.

She had gone one day to his home with a message from Miss Lane to the housekeeper and, finding no one at home in the house, had crossed the yard to a shed where Willie was working. He was sorting out planks and, intending to tease and perhaps to shock her, he showed her a pile at the farther end of the shed in the semi-darkness. 'Just look at these,' he said. 'Here! Come right in and put your hand on them. Know what they're for? Well, I'll tell you. They're all and every one of them sides for coffins. I wonder who this one's for, and this and this. This nice little narrow one may be for you; it looks about the right size. And this one at the bottom' – touching it with his toes – 'may be for that very chap we can hear kicking up such a row with his whistling outside. They're all booked for somebody, mostly somebody we know, but there aren't any names written on them.'

Laura pretended to laugh and called him a horrid boy, but the bright day seemed to her suddenly to become dark and cold, and, afterwards, whenever she passed that shed she shivered and thought of the pile of coffin boards waiting in the half-darkness until they should be needed to make coffins for people now going happily about the green on their business and passing the shed without a shudder. The elm or the oak which had yet to make her coffin must then have been growing green, somewhere or other, and Willie had no coffin tree growing for him, for his was a soldier's grave out on the veld in South Africa.

He, the youngest, was the first of the three Williams to go. Soon after, the middle William died suddenly while working at his bench, and his father followed him next winter. Then the carpenters' shop was demolished to make way for a builder's showroom with baths and tiled fireplaces and w.c. pans in the window, and only the organ in church and pieces of good woodwork in houses remained to remind those who had known them of the three Williams.

Squeezed back to leave space for a small front garden, between the Stores and the carpenters' shop, was a tall, narrow cottage with three sash windows, one above the other, which almost filled the front wall. In the lowest window stood a few bottles of bullseyes and other boiled sweets, and above them hung a card which said: *Dressmaking and Plain Sewing*. This was the home of one of the two postwomen who, every morning, carried the letters to outlying houses off the regular postman's beat.

Unlike her colleague, who was old, grumpy and snuffy, Mrs Macey was no ordinary countrywoman. She spoke well and had delicate, refined, if somewhat worn, features, with nice grey eyes and a figure of the kind of which country people said: 'So-and-So'd manage to look well-dressed if she went round wrapped in a dish-cloth.' And Mrs Macey did manage to look well-dressed, although her clothes were usually shabby and sometimes peculiar. For most of the year on her round she wore a long grey cloth coat of the kind then known as an 'ulster', and, for headgear, a man's black bowler hat draped with a black lace veil with short ends hanging at the back. This hat, Miss Lane said, was a survival of a fashion of ten years before. Laura had never seen another like it, but worn as Mrs Macey wore it, over a head of softly waving dark hair drawn down into a little tight knob on the neck, it was decidedly becoming. Instead of plodding or sauntering country fashion, Mrs Macey walked firmly and quickly, as if with a destination in view.

Excepting Miss Lane, who was more of a patron than a friend, Mrs Macey had no friends in the village. She had been born and had lived as a child on a farm near Candleford Green where her father was then bailiff; but before she had grown up her family had gone away and all that was known locally of fifteen years of her life was that she had married and lived in London. Then, four or five years before Laura knew her, she had returned to the village with her only child, at that time a boy of seven, and taken the cottage next to the Stores and put the card in the window. When the opportunity offered, Miss Lane obtained for her the letter-carrier's post and, with the four shillings a week pay for that, a weekly postal order for the same amount from some mysterious organization (the Freemasons, it was whispered, but that was a mere guess) and the money earned by her sewing, she was able in those days and in that locality to live and bring up her boy in some degree of comfort.

She was not a widow, but she never mentioned her husband unless questioned, when she would say something about 'travelling abroad with his gentleman', leaving her hearer to conclude that he was a valet or something of that kind. Some people said she had no husband and never had had one, she had only invented one as a blind to account for her child, but Miss Lane nipped such suspicions in the bud by saying authoritatively that she had good reasons which she was not at liberty to reveal for saying that Mrs Macey had a husband still living.

Laura liked Mrs Macey and often crossed the green to her house in the evening to buy a screw of sweets or to try on a garment which was being made or turned or lengthened for her. It was as cosy a little place as can be imagined. The ground floor of the house had formerly been one largish room with a stone floor, but, by erecting a screen to enclose the window and fireplace and cut off the draughty outer portion, where water vessels and cooking utensils were kept, Mrs Macey had contrived a tiny inner living-room. In this she had a table for meals, a sofa and easy chair, and her sewing-machine. There were rugs on the floor and pictures on the walls and plenty of cushions about. These were all of good quality – relics, no doubt, of the much larger home she had had during her married life.

There Laura would sit by the fire and play ludo with Tommy, with Snowball, the white cat, on her knee, while Mrs Macey, on the other side of the hearth, stitched away at her sewing. She did not talk much, but she would sometimes look up and her eyes would smile a welcome. She seldom smiled with her lips and scarcely ever laughed and, because of this, some villagers called her 'sour-looking'. 'A sour-looking creature,' they said, but any one with more penetration would have known that she was not sour, but sad. 'Ah! you're young!' she once said when Laura had been talking a lot. 'You've got all your life before you!' as though her own life was over, although she was not much over thirty.

Her Tommy was a quiet, thoughtful little lad with the man-of-the-house air of responsibility sometimes worn by fatherless only sons. He liked to wind up the clock, let out the cat, and lock the house door at night. Once when he had brought home a blouse which Mrs Macey had been making out of an old muslin frock for Laura and with it the bill, for some now incredibly small amount – a shilling at the most, probably ninepence – Laura, by way of a mild joke, handed him her pencil and said, 'Perhaps you'll give me a receipt for the money?' 'With pleasure,' he said in his best grown-up manner. 'But it's really not necessary. We shan't charge you for it again.' Laura smiled at that 'we', denoting a partnership in which the junior partner was so very immature, then felt sad as she thought of the two of them, entrenched in that narrow home against the world with some mysterious background which could be felt but not fathomed.

Whatever the nature of the mystery surrounding the father, the boy knew nothing about it, for twice in Laura's presence he asked his mother, 'When will our Daddy come home?' and his mother, after a long pause, replied: 'Oh, not for a long time yet. He's travelling abroad, you know, and his gentleman's not ready to come home.' The first time she added, 'I expect they're shooting tigers', and the next, 'It's a long way to Spain.'

Once Tommy, in all innocence, brought out and showed Laura his father's photograph. It was that of a handsome, flashy-looking man posing before the rustic-work background of a photographer's studio. A top-hat and gloves were carefully arranged on a little table beside him. Not a working man, evidently, and yet he did not look quite like a gentleman, thought Laura, but it was no business of hers, and when she saw Mrs Macey's pained look as she took away the photograph she was glad that she had barely glanced at it.

At one end of the green, balancing the doctor's house at the other end, stood what was known there as a quality house, which meant one larger than a cottage, but smaller than a mansion. There were several such houses in the neighbourhood of Candleford Green, mostly occupied by ladies, elderly maiden or widowed, but here there lived only one gentleman. It was a white house with a green-painted balcony, green outside shutters, and a beautifully kept lawn with clipped yew trees. It was a quiet house, for Mr Repington was a very old gentleman and there were no young people to run in and out or to go to parties or hunting. His maidservants were elderly and uncommunicative, and his own man, Mr Grimshaw, was as white-headed as his master and as unapproachable.

Sometimes, on summer afternoons, a carriage with champing horses, glittering harness, and cockaded coachman and footman would stand at the gate, while, from within, through the open windows, came the sounds of tinkling teacups and ladies' voices, gossiping pleasantly, and every year, at strawberry time, Mr Repington gave one garden party to which the local gentlepeople came on foot because his stabling accommodation and that of the inn was strained to the utmost by the equipages of guests from farther afield. That was all he did in the way of entertaining. He had long given up dining out or dining others, on account of his age.

Every morning, at precisely eleven o'clock, Mr Repington would emerge from his front door, held ceremoniously open for him by Grimshaw, visit the Post Office and the carpenters' shop, stand for a few minutes to talk to the Vicar or any one else of his own class whom he happened to meet, pat a few children on the head and give a knob of sugar to the donkey. Then, having made the circuit of the green, he would disappear through his own doorway and be seen no more until the next morning.

His dress was a model of style. The pale grey suits he favoured in summer always looked fresh from the tailor's hand, and his spats and grey suède gloves were immaculate. He carried a gold-headed cane and wore a flower in his button-hole, usually a white carnation or a rosebud. Once when he met Laura out in the village he swept off his panama hat in a bow so low that she felt like a princess. But his manners were always courtly. It was not at all surprising to be told that he had formerly held some position at the Court of Queen Victoria. Which perhaps he had, perhaps not, for nothing was really known about him, excepting that he was apparently rich and obviously aged. Laura and Miss Lane knew and the postman may have noticed that he had many letters with crests and coronets on the flap of the envelope, and Laura knew that he had once sent a telegram signed with his Christian name to a very great personage indeed. But, his servants being what they were, such things were not matter for village gossip.

Like all those of good birth Laura met when in business, his voice was quiet and natural, and he was pleasant in his manner towards her. One morning he found her alone in the office, and perhaps intending to cheer what he may have thought her loneliness, he asked: 'Do you like ciphers?' Laura was not at all sure what kind of a cipher he meant – it could not be the figure nought, surely – but she said, 'Yes, I think so,' and he wrote with a tiny gold pencil on a leaf torn from his pocket-book:

U O A O, but I O thee.
I give thee A O, but O O me,

which, seeing her puzzled look, he interpreted:

> 'You sigh for a cipher, but I sigh for thee
> I give thee a cipher, but O sigh for me.'

And, on another occasion, he handed her the riddle:

> The beginning of Eternity,
>   The end of Time and Space,
> The beginning of every end
>   And the end of every place,

to which she soon discovered that the answer was the letter 'E'.

Laura wondered in riper years how many times and in how many different environments he had written those very puzzles to amuse other girls, unlike her in everything but age.

There were a number of small cottages around the green, most of them more picturesque than that occupied by Mrs Macey. Of these Laura knew every one of the occupants, at least well enough to be on speaking terms, through seeing them at the post office. She did not know them as intimately as she had known similar families in her native hamlet, where she had been one of them and had had a lifelong experience of their circumstances. At Candleford Green she was more in the position of an outside observer aided by the light of her previous experiences. They appeared to have a similar home life to that of the Lark Rise people, and to possess much the same virtues, weaknesses, and limitations. They spoke with the same country accent and used many of the old homely expressions. Their vocabulary may have been larger, for they had adopted most of the new catchwords of their day, but, as Laura thought afterwards, they used it with less vigour. One new old saying, however, Laura heard for the first time at Candleford Green. It was used on an occasion when a woman, newly widowed, had tried to throw herself into her husband's grave at his funeral. Then some one who had witnessed the scene said dryly in Laura's hearing: 'Ah, you wait. The bellowing cow's always the first to forget its calf.'

The Candleford Green workers lived in better cottages and many of them were better paid than the Lark Rise people. They were not all of them farm labourers; there were skilled craftsmen amongst them, and some were employed to drive vans by the tradesmen there and in Candleford town. But wages for all kinds of work were low and life for most of them must have been a struggle.

The length of raised sidewalk before the temptingly dressed windows of the Stores was the favourite afternoon promenade of the women, with or without perambulators. There *The Rage* or *The Latest*, so ticketed, might be seen free of charge, and the purchase of a reel of cotton or a paper of pins gave the right of entry to a further display of fashions. On Sundays the two Misses Pratt displayed the cream of their stock upon their own persons in church. They were tall, thin young women with frizzy Alexandra fringes of straw-coloured hair, high cheek-bones and anaemic complexions which they touched up with rouge.

At the font they had been given the pretty, old-fashioned names of Prudence and Ruth, but for business purposes, as they explained, they had exchanged them for the more high-sounding and up-to-date ones of Pearl and Ruby. The new names passed into currency sooner than might have been expected, for few of their customers cared to offend them. They might have retaliated by passing off on the offender an unbecoming hat or by skimping the sleeves of a new Sunday gown. So, to their faces, they were 'Miss Pearl' and 'Miss Ruby', while, behind their backs, as often as not, it would be 'That Ruby Pratt, as she calls herself ', or 'Pearl as ought to be Prudence'.

Miss Ruby ran the dressmaking department and Miss Pearl reigned in the millinery showroom. Both were accepted authorities upon what was being worn and the correct manner of wearing it. If any one in the village was planning a new summer outfit and was not sure of the style, she would say, 'I must ask the Miss Pratts,' and although some of the resulting creations might have astonished leaders of fashion elsewhere, they were accepted by their customers as models. In Laura's time the Pratts' customers included the whole feminine population of the village, excepting those rich enough to buy elsewhere and those too poor to buy at all at first-hand.

Flora Thompson

They were good enough girls, enterprising, hard-working, and clever, and if Laura thought them conceited, that may have been because she had been told that Miss Pearl had said to a customer in the showroom that she wondered that Miss Lane had not been able to find some one more genteel than that little country girl to assist her in her office.

At the time of her marriage, it was said, their mother had been looked upon as an heiress, having not only inherited the Stores, then a plain draper's shop with rolls of calico and red flannel in the window, but also cottages and grazing land, bringing in rent, so it may be supposed she felt justified in marrying where her fancy led her. It led her to marriage with a smart young commercial traveller whose round had brought him to the shop periodically, and together they had introduced modern improvements.

When the new plate-glass windows had been put in, the dress-making and millinery departments established, and the shop renamed 'The Stores', the husband's efforts had ended, and for the rest of his life he had felt himself entitled to spend most of his waking hours in the bar parlour of the 'Golden Lion' laying down the law to other commercial gentlemen who had not done so well for themselves. 'There goes that old Pratt again, shaking like a leaf and as thin as a hurdle,' Miss Lane would say when taking her morning survey of the green from her window, and Laura, glancing up from her work, would see the thin figure in loud tweeds and white bowler hat making for the door of the inn and know, without looking at the clock, that it was exactly eleven. Some time during the day he would go home for a meal, then return to his own special seat in the bar parlour, where he would remain until closing time.

At home his wife grew old and shrivelled and complaining, while the girls grew up and shouldered the business, just in time to stop its decline. At the time Laura knew them their 'Ma', as her daughters called her, had become an invalid on whom they lavished the tenderest care, obtaining far-fetched dainties to tempt her appetite, filling her room with flowers, and staging there a private show of their latest novelties before they were displayed to the public. 'No. Not that one, please, Mrs Perkins,' Miss Pearl said to a customer in

74

Laura's hearing one day. 'I'm ever so sorry, but it's the new fashion, only just come in, and Ma's not seen it yet. I'd take it upstairs now to show her, but she takes her little siesta at this hour. Well, if you really don't *mind* stepping round again in the morning . . .'

If, through absent-mindedness or a lost sense of direction, Pa wandered in his hat and coat into the showroom, he was gently but firmly led out by a seemingly playful daughter. 'Dear Papa!' Miss Pearl would exclaim. 'He does take such an interest. But come along, darling. Come with your own little Pearlie. Mind the step, now! Gently does it. What you want is a nice strong cup of tea.'

No wonder the Pratt girls looked, as some people said, as if they had the weight of the world on their shoulders. They must in reality have carried a biggish burden of trouble, and if they tried to hide it with a show of high spirits and simpering smiles, plus a little harmless pretension, that should have been put down to their credit. Human nature being what it is, their shifts and pretences only served to provoke a little mild amusement. But, by the time Laura went to live at Candleford Green the Pratts' was an old story, until, one summer morning, a first-class sensation was provided for the villagers by the news that Mr Pratt had disappeared.

He had left the inn at the usual time, closing time, but had never reached home. His daughters had sat up for him, gone after midnight to the 'Golden Lion' to inquire, and then headed the search in the lanes in the early dawn, but there was still no trace, and the police were about, asking questions of early workmen. Would they circulate his photograph? Would there be a reward? And, above all, what had become of the man? 'Thin as he was, he couldn't have fallen down a crack, like!'

The search went on for days. Stationmasters were questioned, woods were searched foot by foot, wells and ponds were dragged, but no trace could be found of Mr Pratt, dead or alive.

Ruby and Pearl, their first grief abating, took counsel with friends as to whether or not to wear mourning. But, no, they decided. Poor Pa might yet return, and they compromised by appearing in church in lavender frocks with touches of mauve, half, or perhaps quarter, mourning. As time went on, the back door, which, so far, had been left on the latch at night in case of the return of the prodigal father, was again locked, and perhaps, when alone with Ma, they admitted with a sigh that all might be for the best.

But they had not heard the last of poor Pa. One morning, nearly a year later, when Miss Ruby had got up very early and, the maid still being in bed, had herself gone to the woodshed for sticks to boil a kettle to make tea, she found her father peacefully sleeping on a bed of brushwood. Where he had been all those months he could not or would not say. He thought, or pretended to think, that there had been no interval of time, that he had come home as usual from the 'Golden Lion' the night before he was found and, finding the door locked and not liking to disturb the household, had retired to the woodshed. The one and only clue to the mystery, and that did not solve it, was that in the early dawn of the day before that of his reappearance a cyclist on the Oxford road, a few miles out of that city, had passed on the road a tall, thin elderly man in a deerstalker cap walking with his head bent and sobbing.

Where he had been and how he had managed to live while he was away was never found out. He resumed his visits to the 'Golden Lion' and his daughters shouldered their burden again. By them the episode was always afterwards referred to as 'Poor Pa's loss of memory'.

The grocer's business next door to the Pratts was also a thriving and long-established one. From a business point of view, 'Tarman's' had one advantage over the Stores, for while the draper's depended chiefly on the middle state of village society, the poor not being able to afford to buy their models and the gentry despising them, the grocer catered for all. At that time the more important village people, such as the doctor and clergyman, bought their provisions at the village shops as a matter of principle. They would have thought it mean to go further afield for the sake of saving a few shillings, and even the rich who spent only part of the year at their country houses or their hunting boxes believed it to be their duty to give the local tradesmen a turn. If there happened to be more businesses than one of a kind in a village, orders were placed with each alternately. Even Miss Lane had two bakers, one calling one week and the other the next, but in her case it may have been more a matter of business than of principle, as both bakers had horses to be shod.

This custom of local dealing benefited all the inhabitants. The shopkeeper was able to keep more varieties of goods in stock and often of a better quality then he would otherwise have done, his cheerful, well-lighted shop brightened the village street, and he himself made enough money in the way of profit to enable him to live in substantial comfort. A grocer had to be a grocer then, for his goods did not come to him in packets, ready to be handed over the counter, but had to be selected and blended and weighed out by himself, and for quality he was directly responsible to his customers. The butcher, too, received no stiff, shrouded carcasses by rail, but had to be able to recognize the points in the living animal at the local market sufficiently quickly and well to be able to guarantee the succulent joints and the old-fashioned chops and steaks would melt in the mouth. Even his scrag ends of mutton and sixpen'orth of pieces of beef which he sold to the poor were tasty and rich with juices which the refrigerator seems to have destroyed in present-day meat. However, we cannot have it all ways, and most villagers would agree that the attractions of films and wireless and dances and buses to town, plus more money in the pocket, outweigh the few poor creature comforts of their grandparents.

Above the grocer's shop, in their large, comfortable rooms, lived the grocer, his wife, and their growing-up family. This family was not liked by all; some said they had ideas above their station in life, chiefly because the children were sent to boarding-school; but practically every one dealt at their shop, for not only was it the only grocery establishment of any size in the place, but the goods sold there could be relied upon.

Mr Tarman was a burly giant in a very white apron. When he leaned forward and rested his hands on the counter to speak to a customer, the solid mahogany seemed to bend beneath the strain. His wife was what was called there 'a little pennicking bit of a woman'; small and fair and, by that time, a little worn, though still priding herself upon her complexion, which she touched with nothing but warm rain water. In spite of the fine lines round her mouth and eyes, which the rain water had not been able to prevent, the effect justified her faith in its efficiency, for her cheeks were as fresh and delicately tinted as those of a child. She was a generous, open-handed creature who gave liberally to every good cause. The poor had cause to bless her, for their credit there in bad times was unlimited, and many families had a standing debt on her books that both debtor and creditor knew could never be paid. Many a cooked ham-bone with good picking still left on it and many a hock-end of bacon were slipped by her into the shopping baskets of poor mothers of families, and the clothes of her children when new were viewed by appraising eyes by those who hoped to inherit them when outgrown.

By neighbours of her own class she was said to be extravagant, and perhaps she was. Laura ate strawberries and cream for the first time at her table, and her own clothes and those of her girls were certainly not bought at the Miss Pratts'.

The baker and his wife were chiefly remarkable for their regularity in adding a new unit to their family every eighteen months. They already had eight children and the entire energies of the mother and any margin the father might have left after earning their living were devoted to nursing the younger and keeping in order the elder members of their brood. But theirs was a cheerful, happy-go-lucky household. The only dig ill-natured neighbours could get in at Mrs Brett was the old one then often heard by young mothers: 'Ah! You wait! They makes your arms ache now, but they'll make your heart ache when they get older.'

The parents were too old and too otherwise engaged and the children were too young to be friends for Laura, and she never heard what became of them; but it would not be surprising to learn that those healthy, intelligent, if somewhat unmanageable Brett children all turned out well.

There were a few other, lesser shops around the green, including the one which was really a cottage where an old dame sold penny plates of cooked prunes and rice to the village boys in the evening. She also made what was known as sticky toffee, so soft it could be pulled out in lengths, like elastic. She took snuff so freely that no one over twelve years of age would eat this.

But we must return to the Post Office, where Laura in the course of her duties was to come to know almost every one.

VI

At the Post Office

Sometimes Sir Timothy would come in, breathing heavily and mopping his brow if the weather were warm. 'Ha! ha!' he would say. 'Here is our future Postmistress-General. What is the charge for a telegram of thirty-three words to Timbuctu? Ah! I thought so. You don't know without looking it up in a book, so I'll send it to Oxford instead and hope you'll be better informed next time I ask you. There! Can you read my handwriting? I'm dashed if I can always read it myself. Well, well. Your eyes are young. Let's hope they'll never be dimmed with crying, eh, Miss Lane? And I see you are looking as young and handsome as ever yourself. Do you remember that afternoon I caught you picking cowslips in Godstone Spinney? Trespassing, you were, trespassing; and I very properly fined you on the spot, although not as yet a J.P. – not by many a year. I let you off lightly that time, though you made such a fuss about a mere –'

'Oh, Sir Timothy, how you do rake up things! And I wasn't trespassing, as you very well knew; it was a footpath your father ought never to have closed.'

'But the game birds, woman, the game birds –' And, if no one else happened to come in, they would talk on of their youth.

For Lady Adelaide, Sir Timothy's wife, the footman usually did business while she sat in her carriage outside, but occasionally she herself would come rustling in, bringing with her a whiff of perfume, and sink languidly down in the chair provided for customers on their side of the counter. She was a graceful woman, and it was a delight to watch her movements. Laura, who sat behind her in church, admired the way she knelt for the prayers, not plumping down squarely with one boot-sole on each side of a substantial posterior, as most other women of her age did, but slanting gracefully forward with the sole of one dainty shoe in advance of the other. She was tall and thin and, Laura thought, aristocratic-looking.

For some time she took no more notice of Laura than one would now of an automatic stamp-delivering machine. Then, one day, she did her the honour of personally inviting her to join the Primrose League, of which she was a Dame and the chief local patroness. A huge fête, in which branches from the surrounding villages joined, was held in Sir Timothy's park every midsummer, and there were day excursions and winter-evening entertainments for the benefit of Primrose League members. It was no wonder the pretty little enamelled primrose badge, worn as a brooch or lapel ornament, was so much in evidence at church on Sundays.

But Laura hesitated and grew red as a peony. In view of her Ladyship's graciousness, it seemed churlish to refuse to join; but what would her father, a declared Liberal in politics and an opponent of all that the Primrose League stood for, say if she went over to the enemy?

And she herself did not really wish to become a member; she never did wish to do what everybody else was doing, which showed she had a contrary nature, she had often been told, but it was really because her thoughts and tastes ran upon different lines than those of the majority.

The lady looked her in the face, her expression showing more interest than formerly. Perhaps she noticed her embarrassment, and Laura, who admired her sincerely and wanted to be liked by her, was about to cave in when 'Dare to be a Daniel!' said an inward voice. It was a catchword of the moment derived from the Salvation Army hymn, 'Dare to be a Daniel. Dare to stand alone', and was more often used as a laughing excuse for refusing a glass of beer in company or adopting a new style of hairdressing than seriously as a support to conscience; but it served.

'But we are Liberals at home,' said Laura apologetically, and, at that, the lady smiled and said kindly: 'Well, in that case, you had better ask your parents' permission before joining,' and that was the end of the matter as far as she was concerned. But it was a landmark in Laura's mental development. Afterwards she laughed at herself for daring to be a Daniel on so small a matter. The mighty Primrose League, with its overwhelming membership, was certainly not in need of another small member. Her Ladyship, she realized, had asked her to join out of kindness, in order that she might qualify for a ticket for the approaching celebrations, and had probably already forgotten the episode. It was better to say clearly and simply just what one meant, whoever one was talking to, and always to remember that what one said was probably of no importance whatever to one's listener.

That was the only decided stand Laura ever took in party politics. For the rest of her life she was too ready to admire the good and to detest what she thought the bad points in all parties to be able to adhere to any. She loved the Liberals, and afterwards the Socialists, for their efforts to improve the lot of the poor. Stories and poems of hers appeared before the 1914 War in the *Daily Citizen*, and, after the war, her poems were among the earliest to appear in the *Daily Herald* under Mr Gerald Gould's literary editorship; but, as we know on good authority, 'every boy and every girl that's born into this world alive, Is either a little Liberal, Or else a little Conserv*ative*', and, in spite of her early training, the inborn cast of her mind, with its love of the past and of the English countryside, often drew her in the opposite direction.

A frequent caller at the Post Office was an old Army pensioner named Benjamin Trollope, commonly called 'Old Ben'. He was a tall, upright old fellow, very neat and well-brushed in appearance, with a brown wrinkled face and the clear, straight gaze often seen in ex-Service men. He kept house with an old companion-in-arms in a small thatched cottage outside the village, and their bachelor establishment might have served as a model of order and cleanliness. In their garden the very flowers looked well-drilled, geraniums and fuchsias stood in single file from the gate to the doorway, every plant staked and in exact alignment.

Ben's friend and stable-companion, Tom Ashley, was of a more retiring disposition than Ben. He was one of those old men who seemed to have shrunken in stature and, by the time Laura knew them, he had become little and bent and wizened. He stayed mostly indoors and made their beds and curry and cobbled their garments, only coming once a quarter to the Post Office for his Army pension, when, no matter what time of year or what kind of weather, he complained of feeling cold. Ben did the gardening, shopping, and other outdoor jobs, being, as it were, the man of the house while Tom acted as housewife.

Ben told Laura that they had decided to rent that particular cottage because it had jessamine over the porch. The scent of it reminded them of India. India! That name was the key to Ben's heart. He had seen long service there and the glamour of the East had taken hold of his imagination. He talked well, and his talk gave Laura a vivid impression of hot, dry plains, steaming jungles, heathen temples, and city bazaars crowded with the colourful life of the land he had loved and could never forget. But there was something more which he felt, but could not express, sights and scents and sounds of which he could only say: 'It seems to get hold of you like, somehow.'

Once, when he was telling her of a journey he had once made to the hills with a surveying party in some humble capacity, he said: 'I wish you could have seen the flowers. Never saw anything like it, never in my life! Great sheets of scarlet as close-packed as they grasses on the green, and primulas and lilies and things such as you only see here in a hothouse, and, rising right out of 'em, great mountains all covered with snow. Ah! 'twas a sight – a sight! My mate says to me this mornin' when we found it was rainin' and his ague shakin' him again, "Oh Ben," he says, "I do wish we were back in India with a bit of hot sun"; and I said to him, " 'Taint no good wishin', Tom. We've had our day and that day's over. We shan't see India no more." '

It was strange, thought Laura, that other pensioners she knew who had served in India had left that land with no regrets and very few memories. If asked about their adventures, they would say: 'The places have got funny names and its very hot out there. In the Bay of Biscay on the way out every man jack of us was seasick.' Most of them were short-service men, and they had returned cheerfully to the plough-tail. They appeared to be happier than Ben, but Laura liked him best.

One day a man known as 'Long Bob', a lock-keeper on the canal, came in with a small package which he wished to send by registered post. It was roughly done up in soiled brown paper, and the string, although much knotted, was minus the wax seals required by the regulations. When Laura offered him the loan of the office sealing-wax, he asked her to seal and make tidy the package for him, saying that his fingers were all thumbs and he hadn't got no 'ooman now to do such fiddling little jobs for him. 'But maybe,' he added, 'before you start on it, you'd like to have a look at that within.'

He then opened the package and brought forth and shook out a panel of coloured embroidery. It was a needlework picture of Adam and Eve, standing one on each side of the Tree of Knowledge with a grove of flowering and fruiting trees behind them and a lamb, a rabbit, and other small creatures in the foreground. It was exquisitely executed and the colours, though faded in places, were beautifully blended. The hair of Adam and Eve was embroidered with real human hair and the fur of the furry animals of some woolly substance. That it was very old even the inexperienced Laura could sense at the first glance, more by something strange and antique-looking about the nude human figures and the shape of the trees than by any visible sign of wear or decay in the fabric. 'It's very old, isn't it?' she asked, expecting Long Bob to say it had belonged to his grandmother.

'Very old and ancient indeed,' he replied, 'and I'm told there's some clever men in London who'll like to see that pictur'. All done by hand, they say, oh, long agone, before old Queen Bess's day.' Then, seeing Laura all eyes and ears, he told her how it had come into his possession.

About a year before, it appeared, he had found the panel on the towing-path of the canal, carelessly screwed up in a sheet of newspaper. Inspired rather by strict principles of honesty than by any idea that the panel was valuable, he had taken it to the Police

Station at Candleford, where the sergeant in charge had asked him to leave it while inquiries were made. It had then, apparently, been examined by experts, for the next thing Long Bob heard from the police was that the panel was old and valuable and that inquiries as to its ownership were in progress. It was thought that it must have been part of the proceeds of some burglary. But there had been no burglary in that part of the county for several years, and the police could get no information of any more distant one where such an article was missing. The owner was never found, and, at the end of the time appointed by law, the panel was handed back to the finder, together with the address of a London sale-room to which he was advised to send it. A few weeks later he received the, to him, large sum of five pounds which its sale had realized.

That was the recent history of the needlework panel. What of its past? How had it come to lie, wrapped in a fairly recent newspaper, on the canal tow-path that foggy November morning?

Nobody ever knew. Miss Lane and Laura thought that by some means it had come into the possession of a cottage family, which, though ignorant of its value, had treasured it as a curiosity. Then, perhaps, it may have been sent by a child as a present to some relative, or as part of an inheritance from some old grandmother who had recently died. The loss by a child of 'that old sampler of Granny's' would be but a matter of cuffing and scolding; poor people would not dream of making what they called a 'hue and cry' about such a loss, or of going to the police. But this was mere supposition; the ownership of the panel and how it came to be found in such an unlikely place remained a mystery.

The office was closed to the public at eight, but, every year, for several Saturday evenings in later summer, Laura was in attendance until 9.30. Then, as she sat behind closed doors reading or knitting, she would hear a scuffle of feet outside and open the door to one, two, or more wild-looking men with touzled hair and beards, sun-scorched faces, and queerly cut clothes with coloured shirts which always seemed to be sticking out of their trousers somewhere. These were the Irish farm workers who came over to England to help with the harvest. They were keen workers, employed on piecework, who could not afford to lose one of the daylight hours. By the time they had finished work all the post offices were closed, postal orders could not be procured on Sunday, and they had to send part of their wages to their wives and families in Ireland, so, to help them solve their difficulty, Miss Lane had for some years sold them postal orders, secretly, after official hours. Now she authorized Laura to sell them.

Laura had been used to seeing the Irish harvesters from a child. Then some of the neighbours at home had tried to frighten her when naughty by saying, 'I'll give you to them old Irishers; see if I don't, then!' and although not alarmed at the threat beyond infancy – for who could be afraid of men who did no one any harm, beyond irritating them by talking too much and working harder and by so doing earning more money than they did? – they had remained to her strangers and foreigners who came to her neighbourhood for a season, as the swallows came, then disappeared across the sea to a country called 'Ireland' where people wanted Home Rule and said 'Begorra' and made things called 'bulls' and lived exclusively upon potatoes.

Now she knew the Irish harvesters by name – Mr McCarthy, Tim Doolan, Big James and Little James and Kevin and Patrick, and all the other harvesters working in the district. More and more came from farther afield as the knowledge spread that at Candleford Green there lived a sympathetic postmistress who would let a man have his postal order for home after his week's work was done. By the time Laura left the village, the favour had had to be extended to Sunday morning, and Miss Lane was trying to harden her heart and invent some reason for withdrawing the privilege which had become a serious addition to her work.

At the time now recorded there were perhaps a dozen of these Saturday-evening clients. None of the older men among them could write, and when Laura first knew them these would bring their letters to their wives in Ireland already written by one of their younger workmates. But soon she had these illiterates coming stealthily alone. 'Would ye be an angel, Missie darlint, an' write just a few little words for me on this sheet of paper I've brought?' they would whisper, and Laura would write to their dictation such letters as the following:

'*My Dear Wife*, – Thanks be to God, our Blessed Lady and the saints, this leaves me in the best of health, with work in plenty and money coming in to give us all a better winter than last year, please God.'

Then, after inquiries about the health of 'herself' and the children, the old father and mother, Uncle Doolan, Cousin Bridget, and each neighbour by name, the real reason for getting the letter written surreptitiously would emerge. The wife would be told to 'pay off at the shop', or to ask such and such a price for something they had to sell, or not to forget to 'lay by a bit in the stocking'; but she was not to deny herself anything she fancied; she should live like a queen if the sender of the letter had his way, and he remained her loving husband.

Laura noticed that when these letters were dictated there were none of the long pauses usual when she was writing a letter for one of her own old countrymen, as she sometimes did. Words came freely to the Irishman, and there were rich, warm phrases in his letters that sounded like poetry. What Englishman of his class would think of wishing his wife could live like a queen? 'Take care of yourself' would be the fondest expression she would find in his letters. The Irishman, too, had better manners than the Englishman. He took off his hat when he came in at the door, said 'please', or, rather, 'plaze', more frequently, and was almost effusive in his thanks for some small service. The younger men were inclined to pay compliments, but they did so in such charming words that no one could have felt offended.

Many gipsies frequented the neighbourhood, where there were certain roadside dells which they used as camping-grounds. These, for weeks together, would be silent and deserted, with only circles of black ash to show where fires had been and scraps of coloured rag fluttering from bushes. Then one day, towards evening, tents would be raised and fires lighted, horses would be hobbled and turned out to graze, and men with lurchers at their heels would explore the field hedgerows (not after rabbits. Oh, no! Only to cut a nice ash stick with which to make their old pony go), while the women and children around the cooking pots in the dell shouted and squabbled and called out to the men in a different language from that they used for business purposes at cottage doors.

'There's them ole gipos back again,' the villagers would say when they saw blue smoke drifting over the treetops. 'Time they was routed out o' them places, the ole stinkin' lot of 'em. If a poor man so much as looks at a rabbit he soon finds hisself in quod, but their pot's never empty. Says they eat hedgehogs! Hedgehogs! He! He! Hedgehogs wi' soft prickles!'

Laura liked the gipsies, though she did sometimes wish they would not push with their baskets into the office, three or four at a time. If a village woman happened to be there before them she would sidle out of the door holding her nose, and their atmosphere was, indeed, overpowering, though charged as much with the odours of wood-smoke and wet earth as with that of actual uncleanliness.

There was no delivery of letters at their tents or caravans. For those they had to call at the Post Office. 'Any letters for Maria Lee?' or for Mrs Eli Stanley, or for Christina Boswell, they would say, and, if there were none, and there very often were not, they would say: 'Are you quite sure now, dearie? Do just look again. I've left my youngest in Oxford Infirmary,' or 'My daughter's expecting an increase,' or 'My boy's walking up from Winchester to join us, and he ought to be here by now.'

All this seemed surprisingly human to Laura, who had hitherto looked upon gipsies as outcasts, robbers of henroosts, stealers of children, and wheedlers of pennies from pockets even poorer than their own. Now she met them on a business footing, and they never begged from her and very seldom tried to sell her a comb or a length of lace from their baskets, but one day an old woman for whom she had written a letter offered to tell her fortune. She was perhaps the most striking-looking person Laura ever saw in her life: tall for a gipsy, with flashing black eyes and black hair without a fleck of grey in it, although her cheeks were deeply wrinkled and leathery. Some one had given her a man's brightly coloured paisley-patterned dressing-gown, which she wore as an outdoor garment with a soft billy-cock hat. Her name was Cinderella Doe and her letters came so addressed without a prefix.

The fortune was pleasing. Whoever heard of one that was not? There was no fair man or dark man or enemy to beware of in it, and though she promised Laura love, it was not love of the usual kind. 'You're going to be loved,' she said; 'loved by people you've never seen and never will see.' A graceful way of thanking one for writing a letter.

Friends and acquaintances who came to the Post Office used often to say to Laura: 'How dull it must be for you here.' But although she sometimes agreed mildly for the sake of not appearing peculiar, Laura did not find life at the Post Office at all dull. She was so young and new to life that small things which older people might not have noticed surprised and pleased her. All day interesting people were coming in – interesting to her, at least – and if there were intervals between these callers, there was always something waiting to be done. Sometimes, in a few spare moments, Miss Lane would come in and find her reading a book from the parlour or the Mechanics' Institute. Although she had not actually forbidden reading for pleasure on duty, she did not altogether approve of it, for she thought it looked unbusinesslike. So she would say, rather acidly: 'Are you sure you can learn nothing more from the Rule Book?' and Laura would once more take down from its shelf the large, cream, cardboard-bound tome she had already studied until she knew many of the rules word for word. From even that dry-as-dust reading she extracted some pleasure. On one page, for instance, set in a paragraph composed of stiff, official phrases, was the word 'mignonette'. It referred only to the colour of a form, or something of that kind, but to Laura it seemed like a pressed flower, still faintly scented.

And, although such callers as the gipsies and the Irish harvesters appealed to her imagination because they were out of the ordinary, she was even more interested in the ordinary country people, because she knew them better and knew more of their stories. She knew the girl in love with her sister's husband, whose hands trembled while she tore open her letters from him; and the old mother who had not heard for three years from her son in Australia, but still came every day to the Post Office, hoping; and the rough working man who, when told for the first time, ten years after marriage, that his wife had an illegitimate daughter of sixteen and that that daughter was stricken with tuberculosis, said: 'You go and fetch her home at once and look after her. Your child's my child and your home's her home'; and she knew families which put more money in the Savings Bank every week than they received in wages, and other families which were being dunned for the payment of bills, and what shop in London supplied Mrs Fashionable with clothes, and who posted the box containing a dead mouse to Mrs Meddlesome. But those were stories she would never be at liberty to tell in full, because of the Declaration she had signed before Sir Timothy.

And she had her own personal experiences: her moments of ecstasy in the contemplation of beauty; her periods of religious doubt and hours of religious faith; her bitter disillusionments on finding some people were not what she had thought them, and her stings of conscience over her own shortcomings. She grieved often for the sorrows of others and sometimes for her own. A sudden chance glimpse of animal corruption caused her to dwell for weeks on the fate of the human body. She fell into hero-worship of an elderly nobleman and thought it was love. If he noticed her at all, he must have thought her most attentive and obliging over his post-office business. She never saw him outside the office. She learned to ride a bicycle, took an interest in dress, formed her own taste in reading, and wrote a good deal of bad verse which she called 'poetry'.

But the reactions to life of a sensitive, imaginative adolescent have been so many times described in print that it is not proposed to give yet one more description in this book. Laura's mental and spiritual development can only be interesting in that it shows that those of a similar type develop in much the same way, however different the environment.

A number of customers rode up to the Post Office door on horseback. A mounting-block by the doorstep, with an iron hook in the wall above to secure the reins, had been provided for these. But the hook was seldom used out of school hours, for, if boys were playing on the green, half a dozen of them would rush forward, calling: 'Hold your 'oss, sir?' 'Let me, sir.' 'Let me!' and, unless the horse was of the temper called 'froxy', one of the tallest and stoutest of the boys would be chosen and afterwards rewarded with a penny for his pains. This arrangement entailed frequent dashes to the door by the customer to see what 'that young devil' was 'up to', and a worrying haste with the business within, but no horseman thought of refusing the job to a boy who asked for it, because it was the custom. The boys claimed the job and the reward of one penny as their right.

The gentlemen farmers to whom most of the horses belonged had fresh, ruddy faces and breezy manners and wore smartly cut riding breeches and coats. Some of them were hunting men with lady wives, and children away at boarding schools. Their farmhouses were comfortably furnished and their tables well covered with the best of food and drink, for everybody seemed in those days to do well on the land, except the farm labourer. Occasionally the rider would be a stud groom from one of the hunting stables. Then, after doing what little business he had, he would ask for Miss Lane, pass through to the kitchen, from which the chinking sound of glasses would soon proceed. Bottles of brandy and whisky were kept for these in a cupboard called 'the stud-grooms' cupboard'. No one in the house ever touched these drinks, but they had to be provided in the way of business. It was the custom.

The sound of a bicycle being propped against the wall outside was less frequent than that of a horse's hoofs; but there were already a few cyclists, and the number of these increased rapidly when the new low safety bicycle superseded the old penny-farthing type. Then, sometimes, on a Saturday afternoon, the call of a bugle would be heard, followed by the scuffling of dismounting feet, and a stream of laughing, jostling young men would press into the tiny office to send facetious telegrams. These members of the earliest cycling clubs had a great sense of their own importance, and dressed up to their part in a uniform composed of a tight navy knicker-bocker suit with red or yellow braided coat and a small navy pill-box cap embroidered with their club badge. The leader carried a bugle suspended on a coloured cord from his shoulder. Cycling was considered such a dangerous pastime that they telegraphed home news of their safe arrival at the farthest point in their journey. Or perhaps they sent the telegrams to prove how far they really had travelled, for a cyclist's word as to his day's mileage then ranked with an angler's account of his catch.

'Did run in two hours, forty and a half minutes. Only ran down two fowls, a pig, and a carter', is a fair sample of their communications. The bag was mere brag; the senders had probably hurt no living creature; some of them may even have dismounted by the roadside to allow a horsed carriage to pass, but every one of them liked to pose as 'a regular devil of a fellow'.

They were townsmen out for a lark, and, after partaking of refreshment at the hotel, they would play leap-frog or kick an old tin about the green. They had a lingo of their own. Quite common things, according to them, were 'scrumptious', or 'awfully good', or 'awfully rotten', or just 'bally awful'. Cigarettes they called 'fags'; their bicycles their 'mounts', or 'my machine' or 'my trusty steed'; the Candleford Green people they alluded to as 'the natives'. Laura was addressed by them as 'fair damsel', and their favourite ejaculation was 'What ho!' or 'What ho, she bumps!'

But they were not to retain their position as bold pioneer adventurers long. Soon, every man, youth and boy whose families were above the poverty line was riding a bicycle. For some obscure reason, the male sex tried hard to keep the privilege of bicycle riding to themselves. If a man saw or heard of a woman riding he was horrified. 'Unwomanly. Most unwomanly! God knows what the world's coming to,' he would say; but, excepting the fat and elderly and the sour and envious, the women suspended judgement. They saw possibilities which they were soon to seize. The wife of a doctor in Candleford town was the first woman cyclist in that district. 'I should like to tear her off that thing and smack her pretty little backside,' said one old man, grinding his teeth with fury. One of more gentle character sighed and said: ' "T'ood break my heart if I saw my wife on one of they,' which those acquainted with the figure of his middle-aged wife thought reasonable.

Their protestations were unavailing; one woman after another appeared riding a glittering new bicycle. In long skirts, it is true, but with most of their petticoats left in the bedroom behind them. Even those women who as yet did not cycle gained something in freedom of movement, for the two or three bulky petticoats formerly worn were replaced by neat serge knickers – heavy and cumbersome knickers, compared with those of today, with many buttons and stiff buttonholes and cambric linings to be sewn in on Saturday nights, but a great improvement on the petticoats.

And oh! the joy of the new means of progression. To cleave the air as though on wings, defying time and space by putting what had been a day's journey on foot behind one in a couple of hours! Of passing garrulous acquaintances who had formerly held one in one-sided conversation by the roadside for an hour, with a light *ting, ting* of the bell and a casual wave of recognition.

At first only comparatively well-to-do women rode bicycles; but soon almost everyone under forty was awheel, for those who could not afford to buy a bicycle could hire one for sixpence an hour. The men's shocked criticism petered out before the *fait accompli*, and they contented themselves with such mild thrusts as:

> Mother's out upon her bike, enjoying of the fun,
> Sister and her beau have gone to take a little run,
> The housemaid and the cook are both a-riding on their wheels;
> And Daddy's in the kitchen a-cooking of the meals.

And very good for Daddy it was. He had had all the fun hitherto; now it was his wife's and daughter's turn. The knell of the selfish, much-waited-upon, old-fashioned father of the family was sounded by the bicycle bell.

VII

'Such is Life!'

Candleford was a pleasant and peaceful place, but it was no second Garden of Eden. Every now and again, often after months of placidity, something would occur to disturb the even current of village life.

Sometimes these events were sad ones: a man was gored by a bull, or broke his neck by falling from a loaded wagon in the harvest field, or a mother died, leaving a brood of young children, or a little boy playing by the river fell in and was drowned. Such tragedies brought out all that was best in village life. Neighbours would flock to comfort the mourners, to take the motherless children into their own care until permanent homes could be found for them, or to offer to lend or give anything they possessed which they thought might be of use to the afflicted.

But there were other happenings, less tragic, but even more disturbing. A hitherto quiet and inoffensive man got drunk and staggered across the green shouting obscenities, an affiliation case brought unsavoury details to light, a sweetheart of ten years' standing was deserted for a younger and fresher girl, a child or an animal was ill-treated, or the usually mild and comparatively harmless village gossip suddenly became venomous. Such things made the young and inexperienced feel that life was not as it had appeared; that there were hitherto unsuspected dark depths beneath the sunny surface.

Older and more experienced people saw things more in proportion, for they had lived long enough to learn that human nature is a curious mixture of good and evil – the good, fortunately, predominating. 'Such is life!' Miss Lane would sigh when something of the kind came to her ears, and once she continued in the same breath, but more briskly, 'Have another jam tart, Laura?'

Laura was shocked, for she then thought tart and tears should be separated by at least a decent interval. She had yet to learn that though sorrow and loss and the pain of disillusionment must come to all, if not at one time then at another, and those around the sufferer will share his or her sorrow to some extent, life must still go on in the ordinary way for those not directly implicated.

At Candleford Green there was no serious crime. Murder and incest and robbery with violence were to its inhabitants just things read about in the Sunday newspapers – things to horrify and to be discussed and to form theories on, but far removed from reality. The few local court cases were calculated rather to cause a little welcome excitement than to shock or grieve.

Two men were charged with poaching, and as this had taken place on Sir Timothy's estate he retired from the Bench while the case was tried. But not, it was said, before he had asked his fellow magistrates to deal lightly with the offenders. 'For,' he was supposed to have added, 'who's going to stump up to keep their families while they are in gaol if I don't.' Sentence was passed with due regard to Sir Timothy's pocket. That case caused but a mild interest and no dissension. A poacher, it was agreed, knew the risks he was running, and if he thought the game was worth the candle, well, let him take the consequences.

Then there was the case of the man who had systematically stolen pigwash from a neighbour. The neighbour, who kept several pigs on an allotment some distance from his dwelling, had bought and collected the pigwash from an institution in Candleford town. The thief had risen early and fed his own pig from his neighbour's pig-tubs every morning for weeks before the leakage was discovered, a watch set, and he was caught, dipper in hand. 'A dirty, mean trick!' the villagers said. A fortnight in gaol was too short a sentence.

But over the case of Sam and Susan, neighbours quarrelled and friends were divided. They were a young married couple with three small children and had, as far as was known, always lived peaceably together until one evening when a dispute arose between them, in the course of which Sammy, who was a great, strapping fellow, fell upon his frail-looking little wife and gave her a bad beating. When this was known, as it was almost immediately, for such bruises and such a black eye as Susan's cannot long be hidden, there was a general outcry. Not that a wife's black eye was an entirely unknown spectacle in the village, though it was a rare one, most of the village couples being able to settle their disputes, if any, in private, but on account of the relative sizes of the couple. Sammy was so very big and tall and strong and Susie so slight and childish-looking, that every one who heard of or saw the black eye called out at once: 'The great big bully, him!' So far opinion was unanimous.

But Susie did not take her whacking in the ordinary way. Other wives who had in the past appeared with an eye blackened had always accounted for it by saying that they had been chopping firewood and a stick had flown up and hit them. It was a formula, as well understood and recognized as their more worldly sisters' 'Not at home', and good manners demanded that it should be accepted at its face value. But Susan gave no explanation at all of her state. She went in and out of her cottage in her usual brisk and determined way about her daily affairs and asked neither sympathy nor advice of her neighbours. Indeed, several days had passed before it became known that, with her black eye and her bruises still fresh, she had gone to the Police Station at Candleford town and had taken out a summons for Sammy.

Then, indeed, the village had something to talk about, and talk it did. Some people professed to be horrified that a great, strapping young fellow like Sam should have been such a brute as to lay hands on his nice little wife, good mother and model housewife as she was, and far and away too good for him. They thought she did quite right to go to the police. It showed her spirit, that it did! Others said Susan was a shrew; as all those thin, fair-haired, vinegarish little women were bound to be, and nobody knew what that poor fellow, her husband, may have had to put up with. It was nag, nag, nag, they'd be bound, every moment he was at home, and the house kept that beastly clean he had to take off his coal-heaving clothes in the shed and wash himself before he was allowed to sit down to his supper. Two parties sprang quickly into being. To one Sam was a brute and Susan a heroine, and if the other did not actually hold up Sam as a hero, they maintained that he was an ill-used young man and that Susan was a hussy. It was a case of one quarrel breeding many.

But Susan had another surprise in store for them. In due course, Sam came up before the Court and was sentenced to one month's imprisonment for wife-beating. Susan came home from the Court and, still without saying a word as to her intention to any one, packed her three small children into the perambulator, locked up the house, and marched off to Candleford Workhouse, as it appeared she had then the right to do, having no official means of support while her husband was in prison. She could quite well have stayed at home, for the tradesmen would have given her credit and the neighbours would have helped, or she could have gone to her parents' home in a neighbouring village, but she chose her own course. The step lost her many of her warmest supporters, who had been looking forward to standing by her with sympathy and material aid, and caused the opposition to condemn her more fiercely. She said afterwards she did it to shame Sam, and in this no doubt she succeeded, for it must have added to his humiliation to know that his wife and children were chargeable to the parish. But the period spent in the poorhouse must have been punishment to herself as well. It was common knowledge that life in such establishments was not a bed of roses for a respectable young woman.

However, it all ended happily. A sight Laura could never forget was that of the reunited family returning to their home after Sam's sentence had expired. They passed the Post Office, talking amiably together, Sam pushing the perambulator and Susan carrying a string bag containing the few little luxuries they had purchased on their way for their second house-warming. Each of the children clutched a toy, that of the little toddling boy being a tin trumpet which he tootled to let people know they were coming. Afterwards Sammy became a model husband, almost excessively gentle and considerate, and Susan, while still keeping the reins in her own hands, took care not to pull too hard on them for Sammy's comfort.

A family dispute about some land at one time caused great excitement. An old man of the village had many years before inherited from his parents a cottage and a couple of small fields which he had so far enjoyed without question. Then a niece of his, the daughter of a younger brother long dead, put in a claim for part of the land, which she said, ought rightfully to have gone to her father. It was an unsound claim, for the house and land had been left by will to the eldest son, who had always lived at home and assisted his parents in working their smallholding. Eliza's father had been left a small sum of money and some furniture. Apparently she had the notion that while money and furniture could be left by will according to the testator's fancy, land had always to be divided between the sons of a family. Even had it been a just claim, it should, after that lapse of time, have been settled in Court, but Eliza, who was a positive, domineering kind of person, decided to take possession by force.

She was living in another village at the time, and the first intimation her uncle had of her intention was when one morning a party of workmen arrived and proceeded to break down the hedge of one of the fields. They had orders, they said, to prepare the site for a new cottage which Mrs Kibble, the owner of the land, was about to have built. Old James Ashley was a peace-loving man, a staunch Methodist, and much respected in the village, but at such an affront, understandably, his anger flared up and the workmen were quickly sent about their more lawful business. But that was only the beginning of a quarrel which lasted two years and provided much entertainment for those not affected.

About once a week the niece appeared, a tall, rather handsome woman, who wore long, dangling gold earrings and often a red shawl. She always refused to step indoors and talk it over reasonably, as her uncle suggested, but planted herself on the plot she called hers and shouted. She might well have relied on her own voice and human curiosity for an audience, but to make sure of one she had provided herself with an old-fashioned dinner-bell which served both to announce her arrival and to drown any rejoinders made by her opponent. He, poor old man, stood no chance at all in the contest. It was contrary both to his own nature and his religious beliefs to take part in a brawl. He would often go in and shut the door and draw down the blind, hoping, no doubt, that his niece would soon tire of shouting abuse if he appeared to take no notice. If something she said was more than he could bear in silence, he would open the door, poke out his head, and, keeping a firm hold on his temper, make some protestation, but, as whatever he said at such times was drowned by a clanging of the bell, it had little effect on village opinion, and certainly none on his niece's behaviour.

His title to his modest estate was so clear that it was surprising how many of the villagers sided with Eliza. They said it was a shame that before his father's body was cold, old Jim should have seized all the land, when it stood to reason it ought to have been divided. These admired Eliza for her spirit and hoped she would insist upon getting her rights, perhaps also hoping subconsciously that she would continue to provide them with entertainment. More thoughtful and better-informed people maintained that the right was on old Jim's side. 'Right's right, and wrong's no man's right,' they quoted sententiously. In the meantime wrong, plus a dinner-bell, appeared to have the best of it.

But old Jim, though an unworldly man, had no intention of parting with any of his property. When he found that lawyers' letters had no effect upon niece Eliza, he did at last take the case to Court, where it was quickly settled in his favour, and Eliza of the bobbing earrings disappeared from the Candleford Green scene. After that, for a time, life in the village seemed strangely silent.

But such disturbances of the peace were well spaced out and few – too few for the tastes of some people. The one constable stationed at Candleford Green had plenty of leisure in which to keep his garden up to the standard which ensured him his customary double-first at the annual Flower Show for the best all-round collection of vegetables and the best-kept cottage garden. After the bicycle came into general use, he occasionally hauled up before the Bench some unfortunate who had exceeded the speed limit, or had been found riding lampless after lighting-up time; but, still, for three hundred days of the year his official duties consisted of walking stiffly in uniform round the green at certain hours by day and taking gentle walks by night to meet his colleague on point duty.

Though not without a sense of the dignity due to his official position, he was a kindly and good-tempered man; yet nobody seemed to like him, and he and his wife led a somewhat isolated life, in the village but not entirely of the village. Law-abiding as most country people were in those days, and few as were those who had any personal reason for fearing the police, the village constable was still regarded by many as a potential enemy, set to spy upon them by the authorities. In Laura's childhood, she knew a woman who declared that she 'went all fainty, like' at the sight of a policeman's uniform, just as some other sensitive people are supposed to do when they smell a rose, or if a cat enters the room. And small boys had a catch which at that time they shouted from behind hedges at a respectful distance after a policeman had passed them:

There goes the bobby with his black shiny hat
　And his belly full of fat
　And a pancake tied to his nose,

a relic, it is to be supposed, from the days before policemen wore helmets.

Of those other offences which do not come within the scope of the law and yet may destroy the peace of a village, Candleford Green had its share. In those days, when countrywomen read little and the cinema had yet to be invented, the thrills which human nature appears to demand had to be extracted from real life. This demand was abundantly met by the gossips. Candleford Green had several of these talented women who could take some trifling event and so expand, distort, and embroider it that by the time a story had made the round of the village, gathering a little in the way of circumstantial detail here and there, and came at last to the ears of the persons concerned, it would bear so little resemblance to the facts of the case that it was indignantly repudiated.

And, indeed, it was annoying to a proud housewife to be told that people were saying that on a certain day last month she had been compelled to raise money by selling her one easy chair, or that a hire-purchase firm had taken it away in default, when what had really happened was that the easy chair had been carried away to be reupholstered, and, far from being penniless, its possessor had the money saved up and actually in her pocket at that moment to pay for the renovation. And it was still more annoying for a young man to have his sweetheart's recent coldness accounted for by the story going the rounds that he had been seen going into the house of a fascinating young widow. Which he had, not as a victim to her fascination, but to investigate the cause of a smoking chimney which his employer, who was also her landlord, had asked him to see to.

Such stories did no great harm. Those concerned who happened to possess a sense of humour would laugh at them as a pack of lies invented by a few gossiping old women who would have been better employed mending the holes in their stockings. Others would go from house to house trying to track down the originator of the gossip. They never succeeded, though most of those they interviewed were in some measure guilty; but the pursuit served to take off the edge of their indignation.

But every few years at Candleford Green, and no doubt in other such villages, stories no more true to fact were circulated which did definite harm. One such was that a young girl, at home for a time from her place in service, was pregnant. There was no truth whatever in the story. She was anaemic and run down and her kindly employers had sent her home for a few weeks' rest and country air, but soon, not only her supposed condition, but also the name of her seducer, was common talk. She was a modest, sensitive girl and in her then weak condition suffered greatly.

Another outlet for the few who had venomous minds was the sending of so-called comic valentines addressed in disguised hand-writing. The custom of sending daintily printed and lace-bedecked valentines by friends and lovers had by that time died out. Laura was born too late ever to receive a genuine valentine. But what were known as comic valentines were still popular in country districts. These were crude coloured prints on flimsy paper representing hideous forms and faces intended to be more or less applicable to the recipient. A valentine could be obtained suitable to be sent to one of any trade, calling, or tendency, with words, always insulting and often obscene, calculated to wound, and these, usually unstamped, passed through the village post offices in surprising numbers every St Valentine's Eve.

Laura once took one out of the posting-box addressed to herself, with the picture of a hideous female handing out penny stamps and some printed doggerel which began:

> You think yourself so la-di-da
> And get yourself up so grand

and went on to advise her always to wear a thick veil when she went out, or her face would frighten the cows. Underneath the verse was scrawled in pencil: 'Wat you reely wants is a mask.' She thrust it into the fire and told nobody, but for some time all pleasure in her own appearance was spoiled and the knowledge that she had an enemy rankled.

But scandalous gossip and the sending of anonymous valentines was but the work of a few of the evil-minded people such as may always be found in any place. The majority of Candleford Green dwellers were kind, as majorities always are. Education had already done something for village life. The old dark superstitions had gone. Poor, ugly, old lone-living women were no longer suspected of witchcraft, although there was one man still living in the village who firmly believed that he had known a witch in his childhood and that she had caused by her magic all manner of misfortunes. Under the influence of her evil eye children had pined and died, horses had gone lame, cows had slipped their calves, and fires had broken out in rickyards.

A disease known locally as the 'scab' had at that time ravaged the sheepfolds and ruined farmers, and, as old Nanny had been known to collect the scraps of wool torn from the sheeps' backs by the bushes, probably to warm her poor old body in some way, the villagers had held her responsible. They said she burned the wool by night, they had smelt it sizzling when passing her cottage; and, as the wool shrivelled, the sheep upon whose backs it had grown developed the scab. Women who offended old Nanny speedily lost their looks, and sometimes their husbands' affections, or their crockery fell from the shelves and got broken. In fact, as one of his hearers once said, old Nanny seemed to have played the very devil with the place. But that was all long before Laura's time, before her father or mother were born. In the eighteen-nineties in that part of the country ordinary people either disbelieved altogether in witchcraft, or thought it one of the old unhappy things of the past, like the gibbet and transportation.

A few innocent charms and superstitious practices were all that remained of magic. Warts were still charmed away by binding a large black slug upon the wart for a night and a day. Then the sufferer would go by night to the nearest crossroads and, by flinging the slug over the left shoulder, hope to get rid of the wart. Fried mice were still given to children as a specific for bed-wetting. The children were told the mouse was meat and ate it without protest, but with what result is unknown. No one would at a table spoon salt on to another person's plate, for 'help you to salt, help you to sorrow'. After Michaelmas blackberries were unfit for food because on Michaelmas Day the devil dragged his tail over them. If a girl began to whistle a tune, those near her would clap their hands over her mouth, for 'A whistling maid and a crowing hen is no good either to gods nor men'. On the other hand, as far as Laura ever heard, one might walk under a ladder with impunity, for the absence of which inhibition she had cause to be thankful in after years, when the risk of a spattering of paint on one's clothing was a trifle compared to that of stepping off the curb and being run over by the traffic.

The funerals of the country poor were at that time a deeply moving sight. At Laura's home the farmer lent one of his farm wagons, freshly painted in bright reds and blues and yellows, or newly scrubbed, to carry the coffin. Clean straw was spread on the bed of the wagon to prevent jolting, and the tired labourer rode to his last rest as he had during his lifetime so many times ridden home from the harvest field. At Candleford Green, the coffin was carried on a wheeled hand-bier propelled by friends. Both were what was called 'walking funerals', the mourners following the coffin on foot. Sometimes there would be but three or four mourners, perhaps a widow supported by her half-grown children. In other instances the procession was quite a long one, especially if the dead had been aged, when sons and daughters and grandchildren, down to the youngest who could toddle, would follow the coffin, the women in decent if shabby and unfashionable mourning, often borrowed in parts from neighbours, and the men with black crape bands round their hats and sleeves. The village carpenter, who had made the coffin, acted as undertaker, and the cost of the funeral, but £3 or £4, was covered by life insurance. Flowers were often placed inside the coffin, but there were seldom wreaths; the fashion for those came later.

The extravagant expenditure on funerals by those who could least afford it was never a feature of country life. A meal to follow the funeral was certainly provided, and the food then consumed was the best the bereaved could obtain. Those funeral meals of the poor have been much misunderstood and misrepresented. By the country poor and probably by the majority of the poor in towns they were not provided in any spirit of ostentation, but because it was an urgent necessity that a meal should be partaken of by the mourners as soon as possible after a funeral. Very little food would be eaten in a tiny cottage while the dead remained there; evidences of human mortality would be too near and too pervasive. Married children and other relatives coming from a distance might have eaten nothing since breakfast. So a ham, or part of a ham, was provided, not in order to be able to boast, 'We buried 'im with 'am', but because it was a ready-prepared dish which was both easily obtained and appetizing.

Those funeral meals have appeared to some more pathetic than amusing. The return of the mourners after the final parting and their immediate outbursts of pent-up grief. Then, as they grew calmer, the gentle persuasion of those less afflicted that the widow or widower or the bereaved parents, for the sake of the living still left to them, should take some nourishment. Then their gradual revival as they ate and drank. Tears would still be wiped away furtively, but a few sad smiles would break through, until, at the table, a sober cheerfulness would prevail. They had, as they told themselves and the others told them, to go on living, and what greater restoratives have we poor mortals than a good meal taken in the company of loving friends? It is possible that the sherry and biscuits provided in more prosperous households after the funerals of that day were sometimes partaken of by sincere and simple-minded people as a much-needed restorative, and not always in order to provide an opportunity for some Victorian father to utter pompous platitudes while he warmed his hinder-parts before the fire.

Ghost stories and stories of haunted houses were still repeated. A few of the more simple people may have believed they were literally true. Others enjoyed them for the sake of the thrill, as we now enjoy reading mystery stories. The more educated scoffed at them as old women's tales. It was an age of materialism, and those in any measure in touch with current ideas believed in nothing they could not feel, or see, or smell.

Laura's mother was the only person she knew at that time who had an open mind on the subject of the supernatural, and she leaned rather to the side of unbelief. She told her children that she had in her time been told many ghost stories, some of which had almost convinced her that there *was* something outside the range of ordinary earthly life, but, she would say, there was always some little loophole for doubt. Still, nobody on earth knew everything; ghosts might have appeared and might appear again, though, she thought, it was doubtful if any happy spirit would wish to leave the glories of Heaven to wander on the earth on dark, cold, winter nights, and as to those who had gone to the bad place, they would not be given the opportunity.

She was never convinced, one way or the other. Yet she was the one person Laura ever came into close touch with and for whose absolute integrity she could vouch who had had an experience which could only be explained by taking into consideration the possibility of the supernatural. It concerned not the dead, but the dying. Laura had a family of cousins on her mother's side, one of whom had married and lived at that time in a neighbouring village, near her old home. Another sister, also married, lived in yet another village, the two, with Laura's home hamlet, arranged like the three points of a triangle.

One of the sisters, Lily, was at the time very ill, and, for a week or more, the other sister, Patience, had been going daily by a direct route which did not pass Laura's home to help with the nursing, returning at night to her own home duties. But on the morning in question, when about to set out, she had the sudden idea of passing by Laura's home in order to collect the rent of a cottage they owned in the hamlet. The tenant was a reliable one, and it had been decided the night before that the rent-collection could wait. But money is always needed at such times and she probably wished to take some little extra luxury or comfort to her sister. No one knew that she was thus going out of her way and she met no one on the quiet country road between the two places.

She collected the rent, then, having to pass her aunt's cottage, looked in at the door upon her. She found her busy with her weekly ironing and alone in the house except for the small baby in the cradle, her husband being at work and her elder children at school for the day. In reply to her aunt's anxious inquiry, Patience said sadly: 'Very, very, ill. It is only a matter of days now, I'm afraid. She may even go today.'

'Then,' said her aunt, 'I'll come with you,' and, after she had bundled away her ironing and put her infant in the perambulator, they hurried off together without seeing or speaking to anybody. Their way lay for the greater part through fields and across a wild heath, and they still saw no one who knew them or could possibly guess their errand.

In the meantime, as they journeyed, in the village of their destination the nurse was washing and making comfortable the invalid. They were alone in the house, together in the one room. Poor Lily was a little peevish, for she was in a weak state – as it proved, actually dying – and objected to being disturbed by the nurse's ministrations.

'Come, come! You must let me make you look nice. Your sister will be here directly,' said the nurse cheerfully.

'I know,' said Lily. 'I can see her. Aunt Emma is with her. They're just coming over Hardwick Heath and they're picking some blackberries.'

'Oh, no, my dear,' said the nurse. 'You mustn't expect your aunt so early in the day as this. She doesn't even know you're so ill, and she's got her young baby to see to. And they wouldn't be picking blackberries. They'd be hurrying on to see you.'

Shortly afterwards they arrived. And blackberries had been picked, for the aunt, not having had time to take flowers from her own garden, had gathered a little bouquet of harebells and other heath flowers, which she had backed with early-turned yellow and crimson bramble leaves and a few sprays loaded with fruit.

VIII

'Ta-ra-ra-boom-de-ay!'

After she had become accustomed to her new surroundings at Candleford Green, Laura was happier, or at least gayer, than she had been since early childhood. Because of her age, or the overflowing abundance of Miss Lane's table, or because something in the air or the life suited her, her thin figure filled out, a brighter colour appeared in her cheeks, and such an inrush of energy and high spirits took hold of her that she would dance, rather than walk, about the house and garden, and felt she could never tire.

This may have been partly due to her release from home cares. At home she had been a little mother to her younger brothers and sisters and the sharer in many of her mother's perplexities. Now she was the youngest in a houseful of adults, the elder of whom treated her as a child. Miss Lane was, at times, even indulgent to her, calling her 'my chick' and making her presents of small, pretty things, which she knew would please her. The old servant, Zillah, tolerated her when she found that she had now some one at hand willing to run upstairs 'to save her poor feet', or to whisk the washing off the line and bring it indoors when it started to rain, or to creep into the low henhouse to collect the eggs for her. She would still sometimes refer to Laura as 'that lafeting little thing' and tell her to wait until the black ox trod on her toes, and, once, in a very bad-tempered moment, she foretold that 'Our missis'll rue the day when she brought that hoity-toity little piece to live along with her', but that was only because Laura had accidentally left footprints on her newly scoured flagstones. Often she was quite pleasant, and on the whole their relations may be described as a state of armed neutrality.

There was no neutrality about Matthew. As he said, if he liked anybody, he *liked* them; if not, they had better keep out of his way. His liking for Laura took the form of kindly teasing. He quizzed her about her clothes and accused her of altering the shape of her best hat once a fortnight. She had re-trimmed it once and he, happening to come into the kitchen while she was doing it, had asked what she thought she was up to. When she said she was trying to make the crown a little lower, he had offered to take the hat out to the forge and lower the crown with his sledge-hammer on the anvil, and that episode furnished him with a standing joke which he repeated every time Laura appeared in anything new. That is a sample of Matthew's jokes. He had scores of similar ones which he was constantly repeating with the intention of amusing her.

Matthew was a small, bent, elderly man with weak blue eyes and sandy whiskers. No one looking at him would have guessed at his importance in the eyes of the local farmers and landowners. He was a farrier as well as a smith, and such a farrier, it was said, as few neighbourhoods could boast of. Horses, indeed, appeared to be more to him than human beings: he understood and could cure so many of their ailments that the veterinary surgeon had seldom to be sent for by the Candleford Green horse-owners.

A cupboard, known as 'Matthew's cupboard', high up on the kitchen wall, held the drugs he used. When he unlocked it, bottles of all shapes and sizes could be seen; big embrocation bottles, stoppered glass jars containing powder or crystals, and several blue poison bottles, one of which must have held at least a pint and was labelled 'Laudanum'. He would hold this last bottle up to the light, shake it gently, and say: 'A wineglass of this wouldn't do some folks I know much harm. Their headaches and whimseys 'udn't trouble them no more, nor other folks neither.'

That was another of Matthew's jokes. He had no enemies, and, as far as was known, no intimate friends among his own kind. His affections were reserved for animals, especially for those he had cured of some sickness or injury. If a cow had a difficult calving, or a pig went off its food, or an infirm old dog had to be put away, Matthew was sent for. He had a tame thrush which he had found in the fields with a broken wing and brought home to treat. He had succeeded to some extent in mending its wing, but it could still only flutter, not fly, so he bought a round wicker cage for it which he kept hung on the wall outside the back door. He released it every day during his dinner-hour, when it would follow him round the garden, *hoppity-hop*.

The younger smiths, who called Laura 'Missy', had little to say to her in public, but when they met her alone in the garden they would offer to reach her a pear or a greengage, or show her some new flower which had come out, or ask her if she had seen old Tibby's new kittens in the woodshed, blushing the while in a way which delighted Laura, who loved to come soundlessly upon them in her new rubber-soled shoes.

Those new lightweight shoes in which Laura hopped and skipped when she should have walked were the thin black rubber ones with dingy-looking, greyish-black uppers, now known as 'gym shoes'. They were known then by the ugly name of 'plimsolls' and had for some time been popular for informal seaside wear by otherwise well-dressed women and children. Now they had been introduced into country districts as a novelty for summer wear, and men and women and girls and boys were all sporting their 'softs'. They were soon found unsuitable for wear in wet weather and on rough country roads, and newer and smarter styles in buck-skin or canvas superseded them for tennis and croquet, but for a summer or two they were 'all the rage', and the young, hitherto accustomed to stiff, heavy leather shoes, luxuriated in them.

Miss Lane still kept to the old middle-class country custom of one huge washing of linen every six weeks. In her girlhood it would have been thought poor looking to have had a weekly or fortnightly washday. The better off a family was, the more changes of linen its members were supposed to possess, and the less frequent the wash-day. That was one reason why our grandmothers counted their articles of underwear by the dozen. And the underwear then in fashion was not of the kind to be washed out in a basin. It had to be boiled and blued and required much ironing. There may have already been laundries, though Laura never heard of one in that district. A few women in cottages took in washing, but most of it was done at home.

For the big wash at Miss Lane's, a professional washerwoman came for two days, arriving at six o'clock on the Monday morning in a clean apron and sun-bonnet, with a second apron of sacking and a pair of pattens in a large open basket upon her arm. Charwomen, too, carried these baskets, 'in case', as they said – meaning in the hope that something or other would be given them to put into them. They were seldom disappointed.

All day on the two washdays, steam and the smell of soapsuds came in great puffs from the window and door of the small, detached building known as the 'washhouse', and the back yard was flooded with waste water flowing down the gutter to the open drain, while the old washerwoman clattered about in her pattens, or stood at her wooden washtub, scouring and rinsing and wringing and blueing, and Zillah, as red as a turkey-cock and in a fiendish temper, oversaw and helped with the work in hand. Indoors, Laura washed up and got the meals. If Miss Lane wanted anything cooked, she had to cook it herself, but cold food was the rule. A ham or half a ham had usually been boiled a few days before.

Soon, sheets and pillow-cases and towels were billowing in the wind on a line the whole length of the garden, while Miss Lane's more intimate personal wear dried modestly on a line by the hen-house, 'out of the men's sight'. All went well if the weather happened to be fine. If not, very much the reverse. The old country saying which referred to a disagreeable-looking man or woman: 'He' – or she – 'looks about as pleasant as a wet washday' would have lost its full flavour of irony if used in these days.

On the evening of the second washday, the washerwoman departed with three shillings, wages for the two days, in her pocket, and in her basket whatever she had been able to collect. The rest of the week was spent by the family in folding, sprinkling, mangling, ironing and airing the clothes. The only pleasant thing about the whole orgy of cleanliness was to see the piles of snowy linen, ironed and aired and mended, with lavender bags in the folds, placed on the shelves of the linen closet and to know that six whole weeks would pass before the next upheaval.

Laura's modest stock of three of everything was, of course, inadequate for such a period; so, before she had come there, it had been arranged that her washing should be sent home to her mother every week. The clothes Laura sent home one week were returned by her mother the next, so Laura received a parcel from home every Saturday. It had had a cross-country journey in two different carriers' carts, but it still seemed to smell of home.

It was her treat of the week to open it. She would bundle the clean clothes, beautifully ironed and folded as they were, higgledy-piggledy upon her bed and seize the little box or package she always found within containing a few little cakes her mother had baked for her, or a cooked home-made sausage or two, or a tiny pot of jam or jelly, or flowers from the home garden. There was always something.

But before she put the flowers in water or tasted a crumb of the food, she would read her mother's letter. Written in the delicate, pointed Italianate handwriting her mother had been taught when a child by an old lady of ninety, the letter would usually begin, 'Dear Laura'. Only on special occasions would her mother write, 'My own dear,' for she was not demonstrative. After the beginning would come the formula: 'I hope this will find you still well and happy, as it leaves us all at home. I hope you will like the few little things I enclose. I know you have got plenty and better where you are, but you may like to taste the home food', or 'smell the home flowers'.

Then followed the home news and news of the neighbours, all told in simple, homely language, but with the tang of wit and occasional spice of malice which made her conversation so racy. She always wrote four or five pages and often ended her letters with 'My pen has run away with me again', but there never was a word too much for Laura. She kept her mother's letters to her for years and afterwards wished she had kept them longer. They deserved a wider public than one young daughter.

At that time Laura had, as it were, one foot in each of two worlds. Behind her lay her country childhood and country traditions, many of which were still current at Candleford Green. Miss Lane's and several similar establishments also still flourished there; but new ideas and new ways were seeping in from the outer world which was still unknown at Lark Rise, and with these Laura was becoming acquainted through friends she was making of her own age.

Some of these she came to know through talking to them over their post-office business; others through her relatives in Candleford town, or because they belonged to families approved of by Miss Lane. They had most of them been brought up in different circumstances from those of her own childhood and they spoke of 'poor people' and 'cottage people' in a way which grated on Laura; but they were lively and amusing and, on the whole, she enjoyed their company.

When she met one of these girls in the street, she would sometimes be invited to 'Come into the wigwam and have a palaver', and they would go up carpeted stairs into the crowded, upholstered drawing-room over the shop and exchange confidences. Or the friend would play her latest 'piece' upon the piano for Laura and Laura would sit and listen, or not listen, but just sit and take mental notes.

There was a piano in every drawing-room and there were palms in pots and saddle-bags suites of furniture and hand-painted milking-stools and fire-screens, and cushions and antimacassars in the latest art shades; but, beyond bound volumes of the *Quiver* and the *Sunday at Home* and a few stray copies of popular novels, mostly of a semi-religious character, there were no books to be seen. The one father who was a reader remained faithful to those works of Charles Dickens which his parents had taken in monthly parts. Most of the fathers of such families found sufficient reading in their *Daily Telegraph*, and the mothers, on Sunday afternoons, dozed over *Queechy* or *The Wide Wide World*. The more daring and up to date among the daughters, who liked a thrill in their reading, devoured the novels of Ouida in secret, hiding the book beneath the mattresses of their beds between whiles. For their public reading they had the *Girls' Own Paper*.

And that was in the 'nineties, afterwards to be named – by a presumably more innocent generation – the 'Naughty 'Nineties'.

Flora Thompson

The clever, witty, but, oh! so outrageous! books of the new writers of the day were, no doubt, read in some of the large country houses around, and they may even have found their way into rectories; but no whisper of the stir they were making in the outer world of ideas had penetrated to the ordinary country home. A little later, the trial of Oscar Wilde brought some measure of awareness, for was it not said that he was 'one of these new poets'? and it just showed what a rotten lot they were. Thank God, the speaker had always disliked poetry.

The tragedy of Oscar Wilde did nothing to lessen their natural distrust of intellect, but it did enlighten the younger generation in a less desirable manner. There were vices, then, in the world one had not hitherto heard of – vices which, even now, were only hinted at darkly, never described. Fathers for weeks kept the newspapers locked up with their account books. Mothers, when appealed to for information, shuddered and said in horrified accents: 'Never let me hear that name pass your lips again.'

Miss Lane, when asked outright what all this fuss was about, said: 'All I know is that it's some law about two men living together, but you don't want to bother your head about things like that!' 'But what about Old Ben and Tom Ashley?' Laura persisted, and was told that those two innocent old comrades had already had their windows broken with stones after dark. People thought, after that, they would leave the village, but they did not. Whoever heard of old soldiers running away? All that happened was that Tom, who had formerly spent most of his time indoors, went out more, and that Ben's walk made him look more than ever as if he had a ram-rod down his back. It was those who had thrown the stones who slunk round corners when they saw Ben or Tom coming.

But although, until that time, not only out of the main stream of ideas but unaware of its existence, before the decade was ended the Candleford Greenites had a Yellow Book of their own in the form of the all-conquering weekly periodical called *Answers*. Already its green counterpart, *Tit-Bits*, was taken by almost every family, and the snippets of information culled from its pages were taken very seriously indeed. Apparently it gave deep satisfaction to the majority of the younger people to know how many years of an average life were spent in bed and how many months of his life a man spent shaving and a woman doing her hair. 'If all the sausages eaten at breakfast in this country on one Sunday morning were stretched out singly, end to end, how many miles do you suppose they would reach?' one neighbour, newly primed, would ask another. Or, in lighter mood, 'What did the cyclist say to the farmer whose cockerel he had run over?' and, only too often, the answer came pat, for the neighbour had just read *his* copy of *Tit-Bits*. The title of *Tit-Bits* furnished a catchword which could always be used with effect when an unfamiliar taste was discovered or an unfamiliar opinion expressed. Then 'Don't try to be funny. We've read about you in *Tit-Bits!*' said scathingly was, in the slang of the day, 'absolutely the last word'.

The girls Laura saw most of at that time were tradesmen's daughters, living at home, employed only in keeping their fathers' business books or in helping their mothers with the lighter house-work. These were known as the 'home birds'; others belonging to the same families were away from home, earning their own living as shop assistants in one of the big London stores, or as school-teachers or nursery governesses. One was in training as a nursing probationer in a London hospital and another was book-keeper and receptionist at a boarding-house. Tradesmen's daughters no longer went into domestic service, unless one, after an apprenticeship to dressmaking and a second apprenticeship to hair dressing, became a lady's maid. Nor did they associate much with the domestic staffs in the big houses, and this not because of snobbishness, but because their lives and interests ran along different lines. The village social system in which the first footman is paired off with the grocer's daughter and the second footman with the post-office girl as a matter of etiquette belongs to the world of fiction.

The home birds were not all of them content with light house-hold duties and, for pleasure, the choir practices and tea-drinkings and village concerts their mothers in their time had found suf-ficient amusement. A few of the boldest among them were already beginning to talk about their right to live their own lives as they wished. According to them, their parents' old-fashioned ideas were their main obstacle. 'Pa's so old-fashioned. You'd think he had been born in the year dot,' these would say. 'And Mama's not much better. She'd like us to talk prunes and prisms and be indoors by ten o'clock and never so much as look at a fellow before he had shown her a certificate of good character.' Far from feeling under any obligation to those who had brought them up and, as Laura in her inexperience thought, been so generous to them, they seemed to think their parents existed chiefly to give them whatever they happened to wish for most at the moment – one of the new safety bicycles, or a sealskin coat, or an outing to London. The parents, on their side, preached circumspect behaviour, obedience, and gratitude as a daughter's first duties, and many clashes ensued.

'I didn't ask to be born, did I?' one girl reported herself as saying to her father, and his retort, 'No; and if you had you wouldn't have been if I had known as much about you as I do now,' was repeated by her as an instance of the ignorance and brutality with which she had to contend.

'Straining at the leash, I am. Straining at the leash,' said Alma dramatically when telling the story to Laura, and Laura, looking round the pretty bedroom and at the new summer outfit, complete with white kid gloves and a parasol, laid out on the bed for her admiring inspection, thought that, at least, the leash was a handsome one. But she did not say so, for even she, brought up in a harder school, could understand that it must be annoying to be treated as a child at twenty, and to be forbidden to do this or do that because it was 'not the thing', and have to depend for every little thing on a parent's generosity.

But the rebellious daughter was the exception. Most of the girls Laura knew were contented with their lot. They enjoyed helping in the house and making Mama bring it up to date and giving tea-parties and playing the piano. Some of these were of the type then called 'sunbeams in the home': good, affectionate, home-loving girls, obviously created for marriage, and most of them did marry and, there can be no doubt, made excellent wives for their own male counterparts.

Laura cannot be said to have been really popular with any of them. Her Candleford town connections vouched for her to some extent, but her own personal antecedents were too humble and her dress and accomplishments fell too short of their own standards for her to rank entirely as one of themselves. Perhaps she was most valued by them as the possessor of a ready ear for confidences and for what they called 'repartee' – a light, bantering form of conversation then much in fashion. But Laura enjoyed their company, and it was good for her. She no longer looked, as the neighbours at home had sometimes said, as if she had all the weight of the world on her shoulders.

Those were the days of Miss Lotty Collins's all-conquering dance and song, 'Ta-ra-ra-boom-de-ay!' and the words and tune swept the countryside like an epidemic. The air that summer was alive with its strains. Ploughmen bawled it at the plough-tail, harvesters sang it in the harvest field, workmen in villages painted the outside of houses to its measure, errand boys whistled it and schoolchildren yelled it. Even housewives caught the infection and would attempt a tired little imitation of the high kick as they turned from the clothes-lines in their gardens singing 'Ta-ra-ra-boom-de-ay'.

Early in the morning, while dew still roughened the turf of the green, Laura's friend at the grocer's, dusting the drawing-room, at sight of the keys of the open piano, would drop her duster, sink down on the music stool, and from the open window the familiar strain would be wafted:

> Such a nice young girl, you see,
> Just out in Society.
> Everything I ought to be.
> > Ta-ra-ra-boom-de-ay!
> A blushing bud of innocence,
> Pa declares a great expense.
> The old maids say I have no sense,
> But the boys agree I'm just immense,
> > Ta-ra-ra-boom-de-ay! Ta-ra-ra-boom-de-ay!

Then the madness would seize her and she would pirouette about the room and come down with such weight from the high kick that her father, honest tradesman, would call urgently to her from the foot of the stairs to remember the drawing-room was immediately over the shop and customers might come in any moment. But, even he, having worked off his annoyance, would go back to his books or his scales humming between his teeth the prevailing tune.

During the day, when the master's back was turned and the shop for the moment was clear of customers, the young men behind the counter would gather up their white aprons in their hands and kick and dance a parody. Ta-ra-ra-boom-de-ay! Ta-ra-ra-boom-de-ay! Were there such things as death and want and grief and misery in that world? If so, youth possessed a charm to banish them from its thoughts in 'Ta-ra-ra-boom-de-ay'.

It would seem that the silly, light-hearted words of the song fitted the tune to perfection; but they were often 'improved' upon. One version, sung by lounging youths beneath the chestnut tree on the green, perhaps nearer the end of the long run of the song, went:

> Lotty Collins has no drawers.
> Will you kindly lend her yours?
> She is going far away
> To sing Ta-ra-ra-boom-de-ay!

But that was sung with the intention of annoying any girl who might happen to be passing. And she would be annoyed. Shocked, too, to hear such an intimate undergarment mentioned in public, and little think that the garment, under that name at least, would pass with the song.

Laura enjoyed life at Candleford Green. In summer the sun seemed to shine perpetually and the winter flew past before she had done half the things she had saved for the long evenings. She was young and she had gay new friends and nicer clothes than she had ever had before and was growing up and could kick as high as anybody to the tune of 'Ta-ra-ra-boom-de-ay!'

But something within her remained unsatisfied. She had her hours of freedom. Every other Sunday, if Miss Lane could spare her, which was not always, she would dress with care and walk into Candleford town for tea with her relatives. She was welcomed warmly, and the hours she spent with her favourite uncle and aunt were pleasant hours, even though her cousins of her own age were away. She enjoyed the Candleford Green village entertainments and the laughing, high-spirited company of her village friends, and Miss Lane's garden was lovely and green and secluded and she spent many happy hours there. But none of these pleasures seemed entirely to satisfy her. She missed – missed badly and even pined for – her old freedom of the fields.

Candleford Green was but a small village and there were fields and meadows and woods all around it. As soon as Laura crossed the doorstep, she could see some of these. But mere seeing from a distance did not satisfy her; she longed to go alone far into the fields and hear the birds singing, the brooks tinkling, and the wind rustling through the corn, as she had when a child. To smell things and touch things, warm earth and flowers and grasses, and to stand and gaze where no one could see her, drinking it all in.

She never spoke of this longing to any one. She accused herself of discontent and told herself, 'You can't have everything,' but the craving remained until, unexpectedly, it was gratified in fullest measure and in a way which seemed to her to be wholly delightful, though, on this latter point, very few of those she knew were inclined to agree.

IX

Letter-Carrier

One cold winter morning, when snow was on the ground and the ponds were iced over, Laura, in mittens and a scarf, was sorting the early morning mail and wishing that Zillah would hurry with the cup of tea she usually brought her at that time. The hanging oil lamp above her head had scarcely had time to thaw the atmosphere, and the one uniformed postman at a side bench, sorting his letters for delivery, stopped to thump his chest with his arms and exclaim that he'd be jiggered, but it was a fact that on such mornings as this there was bound to be a letter for every house, even for those which did not have one once in a blue moon. 'Does it on purpose, I s'pose,' he grumbled.

The two women letter-carriers, who had more reason than he to complain, for his round was mostly by road and theirs were cross-country, worked quietly at their bench. The elder, Mrs Gubbins, had got herself up to face the weather by tying a red knitted shawl over her head and wearing the bottoms of a man's corduroy trouser-legs as gaiters. Mrs Macey had brought out an old, moth-eaten fur tippet which smelt strongly of camphor. As the daylight increased, the window became a steely grey square with wads of snow at the corners of the panes. From beyond it came the crunching sound of cart-wheels on frozen snow. Laura turned back her mittens and rubbed her chilblains.

Then, suddenly, the everyday dullness of work before breakfast was pierced by a low cry of distress from the younger postwoman. She had an open letter in her hand and evidently it contained bad news, but all she would say in answer to sympathetic inquiries was: 'I must go. I must go at once. Now, immediately.' Go at once? Go where? And why? How could she go anywhere but on her round? Or leave her letters half-sorted? were the shocked questions the eyes of the other three asked each other. When Laura suggested calling Miss Lane, Mrs Macey exclaimed: 'No, don't call her here, please. I must see her alone and in private. And I shan't be able to take out the letters this morning. Oh, dear! Oh, dear! What's to be done?'

Miss Lane was downstairs and alone in the kitchen, with her feet on the fender, sipping a cup of tea. Laura had expected she would be annoyed at being disturbed before her official hours, but she did not even seem to be surprised, and in a few moments had Mrs Macey in a chair by the fire and was holding a cup of hot tea to her lips. 'Come. Drink this,' she said. 'Then tell me about it.' Then to Laura, who had already reached the door on her way back to her sorting, 'Tell Zillah not to begin cooking breakfast until I tell her to,' and, as an after-thought: 'Say she is to go upstairs and begin getting my room ready for turning out,' a message which, when delivered, annoyed Zillah exceedingly, for she knew and she knew Laura would guess that the upstairs work was ordered to prevent listening at keyholes.

The sorting was finished, the postman had gone reluctantly out, five minutes late, and old Mrs Gubbins was pretending to hunt for a lost piece of string in order to delay her own exit when Miss Lane came in and carefully shut the door after her. 'What? Not out yet, Mrs Gubbins?' she asked coldly, and Mrs Gubbins responded to the hint, banging the door behind her as the only possible expression of her frustrated curiosity.

'Here's a pretty kettle of fish! We're in a bit of a fix, Laura. Mrs Macey won't be able to do her round this morning. She's got to go off by train at once to see her husband, who's dangerously ill. She's gone home now to get Tommy up and get ready. She's taking him with her.'

'But I thought her husband was abroad,' said the puzzled Laura.

'So he may have been at one time, but he isn't now. He's down in Devonshire, and it'll take her all day to get there, and a cold, miserable journey it'll be for the poor soul. But I'll tell you more about that later. The thing now is what we are going to do about the letters and Sir Timothy's private postbag. Zillah shan't go. I wouldn't demean myself to ask her, after the disgraceful way she's been banging about upstairs, not to mention her bad feet and her rheumatism. And Minnie's got a bad cold. She couldn't take out the telegrams yesterday, as you know, and nobody can be spared from the forge with this frost, and horses pouring in to be rough-shod; and every moment it's getting later, and you know what old Farmer Stebbing is: if his letters are ten minutes late, he writes off to the Postmaster-General, though, to be sure, he might make some small allowance this morning for snow and late mails. What a fool I must have been to take on this office. It's nothing but worry, worry, worry – '

'And I suppose I couldn't be spared to go?' asked Laura tentatively. Miss Lane was inclined to reconsider things if she appeared too eager. But now, to her great delight, that lady said, quite gratefully, 'Oh, *would* you? And you don't think your mother would mind? Well, that's a weight off my mind! But you're not going without some breakfast inside you, time or no time, or for all the farmers and squires in creation.' Then, opening the door: 'Zillah! Zillah! Laura's breakfast at once! And bring plenty. She's going out on an errand for me. Bacon and two eggs, and make haste, please.' And Laura ate her breakfast and dressed herself in her warmest clothes, with the addition of a sealskin cap and tippet Miss Lane insisted upon lending her, and hurried out into the snowy world, a hind let loose, if ever there was one.

As soon as she had left the village behind, she ran, kicking up the snow and sliding along the puddles, and managed to reach Farmer Stebbing's house only a little later than the time appointed for the delivery of his letters in the ordinary way by the post-office authorities. Then across the park to Sir Timothy's mansion and on to his head gardener's house and the home farm and half a dozen cottages, and her letters were disposed of.

Laura never forgot that morning's walk. Fifty years later she could recall it in detail. Snow had fallen a few days earlier, then had frozen, and on the hard crust yet more snow had fallen and lay like soft, feathery down, fleecing the surface of the level open spaces of the park and softening the outlines of hillocks and fences. Against it the dark branches and twigs of the trees stood out, lacelike. The sky was low and grey and soft-looking as a feather-bed.

Her delivery finished, and a little tired from her breathless run, she stopped where her path wound through a thicket to eat the crust and apple she had brought in her pocket. It was an unfrequented way and the only human footprints to be seen were her own, but she was not alone in that solitude. Everywhere, on the track and beneath the trees, the snow was patterned with tiny claw-marks, and gradually she became aware of the subdued, uneasy fluttering and chirping noises of birds sheltering in the undergrowth. Poor birds! With the earth frozen and the ponds iced over, it was indeed the winter of their discontent, but all she could do for them was to scatter a few crumbs on the snow. The rabbits were better off: they had their deep, warm burrows; and the pheasants knew where to go for the corn the gamekeeper spread for them in such weather. She could hear the *honk* of a pheasant somewhere away in the woods and the cawing of rooks passing overhead and Sir Timothy's stable clock chiming eleven. Time for her to be going!

In spite of a late start and a leisurely return, Laura managed to reach the office only a few minutes later than the official time fixed for that journey, which pleased Miss Lane, as it saved her the trouble of making a report, and that, perhaps, made her more communicative than usual, for, at the first opportunity, she told Laura what she knew of Mrs Macey's story.

Her husband, Laura now learned, was not a valet, although he might at one time have been one; nor was he travelling with his gentleman. He was by profession a bookmaker, which interested Laura greatly, as she at first concluded that he was in some way engaged in the production of literature. But Miss Lane, who knew more of the world, made haste to explain that his kind of bookmaker had something to do with betting on race-horses. In the course of his bookmaking, she said, he had been involved in a public-house quarrel which had led to blows, and from blows to kicks, and a man had been killed. The crime had been brought home to him and he had been given a long sentence for manslaughter. Now he was in prison on Dartmoor, nearing the end of his sentence. A long, long way for that poor soul to go in that wintry weather; but the prison authorities had written to say he was dangerously ill with pneumonia and the prison doctor thought it advisable that his wife should be sent for.

Miss Lane had known all the time where he was, though not what crime had caused him to be there, and she had not breathed a word to a living soul, she assured Laura, and would not be doing so now had not Mrs Macey said, as she went out of the door: 'Perhaps Laura will go over and feed Snowball. I'll pay for his milk when I get back. And tell her whatever you think fit about where we are going. She's a sensible little soul and won't tell anybody if you ask her not to.'

Poor Mrs Macey! No wonder she had been distressed. The strain of the journey in such weather and the ordeal at the end of it were not the whole of her trouble. As far as Tommy knew, his father was a gentleman's servant travelling abroad with his employer. Now, at some point on their journey, she would have to tell him the truth and to prepare him for whatever might follow.

Furthermore, her husband's sentence would expire in a year and, if his conduct had been good, he would be released sooner – unless – unless – well, unless he died now through this illness, which Miss Lane thought would be the best thing that could happen for all parties. Still, a husband was a husband, and often the worst husbands were most mourned for. She would not pretend to say whether his wife would be relieved or sorry if the Lord saw fit to take him. All she could say was that she had never seen a poor creature more upset by bad news, and her heart ached at the thought of her, setting off on such a journey, to the end of the earth, as one might say, and snow on the ground, and a prison hospital and all manner of humiliations at the end of it. However, dinner was ready, and Zillah had made a delicious damson jam roly-poly with a good suety crust. Laura must feel hungry after her cold walk, and she felt a bit peckish herself. 'So come along; and not a word of what you've been told to anybody. If any one asks you, it's her mother who's ill, and she's gone to London to nurse her.'

A week later, Mrs Macey returned, sad and subdued, but not in mourning, as Miss Lane had half-expected. She had spent a night in London and left Tommy with her friends there, for she had only come back to settle up her small affairs and to pack her furniture. Her husband was recovering and would shortly be released, and she had decided to make a home for him, for a husband is a husband, as Miss Lane had so sagely remarked, and although Mrs Macey obviously dreaded the future, she felt she must face it. But she could not let her husband come to Candleford Green to make a nine days' wonder. She would find a couple of rooms near her friends in London, and the Prisoners' Aid people would find him a job, or if not, she could earn their keep with her needle. She was sorry to leave her nice little cottage – she had had a few years' peace there – but, as Laura would find, you can't always do what you like or be where you would wish in this world.

So she went with her boxes and bundles and with Snowball mewing in a basket. Someone else came to live in her cottage and very soon she was forgotten, as Laura, in her turn, would be forgotten, and as all the other insignificant people would be who had sojourned for a time at Candleford Green.

But her going had its effect upon Laura's life, for, after a good deal of discussion among her elders and hopes and fears on Laura's part, it was arranged that she should undertake what was still known as 'Mrs Macey's delivery'. Miss Lane was quite willing to spare her for two and a half hours each morning. She had suggested the plan, pointing out that it would not only give her more fresh air and exercise, but also put another four shillings a week in her pocket.

It was really most generous of Miss Lane; and four shillings a week was considered quite a substantial addition to larger incomes than Laura's in those days; yet Laura, sent home for a week-end to obtain her parents' consent to the arrangement found them less pleased with the plan than she had expected. Except in letters from Laura, neither of them had heard of postwomen before, and the idea of letters being delivered by any one but a man in uniform struck them as odd. Her father thought she would demean herself and get coarse and tomboyish trapesing about the country with a letterbag strapped over her shoulder. Her mother's objection was that people would think it funny. However, as it was Miss Lane's suggestion and Laura herself was bent on the plan, they gave, at last, a grudging consent, her father stipulating that she should keep strictly to her official timetable and favour nobody, and her mother that she should never forget to change her shoes in wet weather.

An order for a pair of stout waterproof shoes at her father's expense was forthwith sent off to her shoemaker Uncle Tom, and it may be recorded here as a testimonial to the old hand-made product that that one pair of shoes outlasted the whole of Laura's time as a postwoman. They might have been worn several years longer had not her taste in shoes changed. They were still well worth the gipsy's fervent 'God bless you, my lady' when exchanged for a basket of plaited twigs filled with moss and ferns.

Laura had been away from the hamlet less than seven months, and nothing appeared to have changed there. The men still worked in the fields all day and worked on their allotments or talked politics at the village inn in the evening. The women still went to the well on pattens and gossiped over garden hedges in their spare moments, and to them the affairs of the hamlet still loomed larger than anything going on in the outside world. They were just as they had been from the day of her birth, yet to her they seemed rougher and cruder than formerly. When they chaffed her about the way she had grown, saying it was plain to see there was plenty to eat and drink at Candleford Green, or commented on her new clothes, or asked her if she had found a sweetheart yet, she answered them so shortly that one good old soul was offended and told her it was no good trying to make strange with one who had changed her napkins as a baby. After that well-merited reproof, Laura tried to be more sociable with the neighbours, but she was young and foolish, and for several years she held herself aloof from all but a few loved old friends when visiting her home. It took time and sorrow and experience of the world to teach her the true worth of the old homely virtues.

But home was still home; nothing had changed there. Her brother had come part of the way to meet her and her two little sisters were waiting on the road nearer home. As they neared the house, with their arms about her, she saw her father, ostensibly examining a branch of a damson tree the last snowstorm had broken, but with an eye on the road. He kissed her with more feeling than he usually displayed. 'Why, Laura!' he exclaimed. 'It's fine to see you!' Then, hastily skirting the sentimentality he detested: 'Quite the prodigal daughter. Well, we haven't exactly killed the fatted calf, for we hadn't one handy, but your mother has killed her very best fowl and it's about done to a turn by this time.'

It was delightful to sit in the familiar room with all the old, familiar things around her, with a fire 'half-way up the chimney', as her mother said, and she usually so frugal. Delightful to have a long secret chat with her brother in the woodshed, to be embraced and made much of by her little sisters and to ride her baby brother on her back round the garden with the wind blowing through their hair.

When her mother called her at five o'clock on the Monday morning to get up and prepare for her long walk back and she tiptoed downstairs and saw the lamplit room and savoured the bacon and potatoes frying for her breakfast, the new interests which had come into her life seemed of small account compared with the permanence of this life at home, to which she felt she belonged. Her father had already gone on his way to work. The children upstairs still slept. For the first time during her visit, she was really alone with her mother.

While Laura ate they conversed in whispers. How glad she was, her mother said, to know she was happy, and how pleased to see her well grown. 'You won't be a little bit of a thing like me. Nobody will ever call *you* a pocket Venus,' which certainly no one was ever likely to do, and that not for reasons of size alone. Then there was news of the hamlet doings, some of it very amusing when told by the speaker, some of it a little saddening, and, at last, they came to Laura's own affairs. First of all, her mother wanted to know why Laura had not been home before. 'Every few weeks,' she reminded her had been the agreement, and she had been away seven months. Miss Lane had kept saying, 'You must wait until we hear of some one going that way to give you a lift,' but to this explanation Laura's mother retorted: 'But what was the matter with walking? You could walk here one day and back the next easily enough, as you are doing now'; to which Laura agreed. She had longed to walk home many a time and had several times suggested that she should, but had never been firm and strong enough to insist in face of Miss Lane's objections.

'You must stick up for your rights, my dear,' said her mother that morning. 'And don't forget what I've always told you; don't try to be clever, or go speaking ill of anybody just to show off your own wit. I know how it is with these clever people, like Dorcas Lane. They think they can see through everybody, and so they can to some degree, but they see so far through people that they sometimes see more than there is there and miss the things that are. And, of course, it was very kind of her to give you that nice fur and fur cap. They'll keep you warm this cold weather. But you don't want to go on accepting a lot of things like that from somebody who, after all, is no relation. You have got your own wages now and can buy what you want, or, if not, we'll buy it for you and if you want any advice as to what to buy or where to buy it, you've got your two aunts in Candleford town.'

Laura blushed again at that, for, although she was supposed to go to see the Candleford relatives on alternate Sundays, she had not been there for weeks. Something had always turned up to prevent her going. Snow or rain, or one of Miss Lane's bad headaches, when she could do no other than offer to get off the Sunday evening mail, though it was not her turn to do so. 'I don't like keeping you from your friends,' Miss Lane would say, 'but I really must lie down for an hour.' Or: 'Really, you can't want to go out in this weather. When you've got off the mail, we'll have a good fire in the parlour and make ourselves cosy and read. Or we might have down that box from upstairs I told you about, and I'll show you the letters my father had from that gentleman about Shakespeare. After all, Sunday's the only day of the week we have to ourselves, with Zillah and the men away.' And, if Laura still looked a little regretful, she would add: 'I believe you think more of your Uncle Tom than you do of me.' Laura did. She thought more of that particular uncle in one way than she did of any one else she knew, for no one else, she felt sure, could equal him in wisdom, wit, and sound, homely common sense. But she was fond of Miss Lane, too, and did not wish to displease her, so she stayed.

She did not attempt to describe to her mother a position she had scarcely begun to realize; but her looks and manner must have betrayed something of it, for her mother repeated: 'You must stand up for your rights, child. Nobody will think any the better of you for making a doormat of yourself. But you'll be all right. You've got a head well screwed on to your shoulders, and a conscience to tell you right from wrong, I should hope'; and they talked of other things until it was time for Laura to go.

Her mother put on her thick cape and walked to the turn of the hamlet road with her. It was a raw, grey winter morning, with stars paling in a veil of cottage chimney smoke. Men, about to start on their way to work, stood lighting pipes at garden gates, or shuffled past Laura and her mother with a gruff 'G'marnin!' Although not frosty, the air was cold and the two snuggled closely together, Laura's arm in her mother's, under the cape. She had grown so much that she had to lean down to her mother, and they laughed at that and recalled the time when she, a tiny mite, had said: 'Some day, when I'm grown up, I'll be the mother and you'll be my little girl.' At the turn of the road they halted and, after a close embrace, her mother said good-bye in the old country words: 'Good-bye. God bless you!'

Then, almost immediately, as it seemed to Laura when looking back, it was spring. The countryside around Candleford Green was richer and more varied than that near her home. Instead of flat, arable fields, there were low, green hills, and valleys and many trees and little winding streams. Her path as postwoman led over much pasture land and she often returned with her shoes powdered yellow with buttercup pollen. The copses were full of bluebells and there were kingcups and forget-me-nots by the margins of the brooks and cowslips and pale purple milkmaids in the water-meadows. Laura seldom returned from her round without more flowers in her hand than she knew what to do with. Her bedroom looked and smelled like a garden, and she stood as many pots and vases about the kitchen as Zillah would permit.

The official time allowance for the journey was so generous that she found that, by walking quickly on her outward way, she could deliver her letters and still have an hour to spare for sauntering and exploring before she need hurry back home. The scheme had evidently been drawn up for older and more sedate travellers than Laura.

Soon she came to know every tree, flower-patch and fern-clump beside her path, as well as the gardens, houses, and faces of the people on her round. There was the head gardener's cottage, semi-Gothic and substantial against the glittering range of glasshouses, and his witty, talkative Welsh wife, kindly, but difficult to escape from; and the dairymaid at the farmhouse who had orders to give her a mug of milk every morning and see that she drank it, because the farmer's wife thought she was growing beyond her strength; and the row of half a dozen cottages, all exactly alike in outward appearance and inside accommodation, but differing in their degree of comfort and cleanliness. Laura wondered then, as she was often to do in her after-life, why, with houses exactly alike and incomes the same to a penny, one woman will have a cosy, tasteful little home and another something not much better than a slum dwelling.

The women at the cottages, clean and not so clean alike, were always pleasant to Laura, especially when she brought them the letters they were always longing for, but seldom received. On many mornings she did not have to go to the cottages, for there was not a letter for any one there, and this left her with still more time to loiter by the pond, reaching out over the water for brandyballs, as the small yellow water-lily was called there, or to brood with her hand over bird's eggs in a nest, or to blow dandelion clocks in the sun. Her uniform in summer was a clean print frock and a shady straw hat, which she would sometimes trim with a wreath of living wild flowers. In wet weather she wore her stout new shoes and a dark purplish waterproof cloak, presented to her by one of her Candleford aunts. She carried a postman's pouch over her shoulder and, for the first part of her outward journey, Sir Timothy's locked leather private postbag.

The only drawbacks to perfect happiness on her part were footmen and cows. The cows would crowd round the stiles she had to get over and be deaf to all her mild shooings. She had been used to cows all her life and had no fear of them in the open, but the idea of descending from the stile into that sea of heads and horns was alarming. She knew they were gentle creatures and would never attack her; but, accidentally, perhaps –. Their horns were so very sharp and long. Then, one morning, a cowman saw her hesitating and bade her, 'Coom on.' If she approached and climbed over the stile quickly, he said the cows would disperse. 'They dunno what you want to be up to. Let 'em see that you've got business on the other side of that stile and that you be in a hurry and they'll make way for 'ee. They be knowin' old craturs, cows.' It was as he had said: when she came to and crossed the stile in a businesslike way, they moved politely aside for her to pass, and they soon became so used to seeing her there that they dispersed at her approach.

The footmen were far less mannerly. At the hour at which she reached the great house every morning, their duties, or their pleasure, lay in the back premises, near the door at which Sir Timothy's postbag had to be delivered. At the sound of the doorbell, two or three of them would rush out, snatch the leather postbag from Laura's hand and toss it from one to the other – sometimes kick it. They hated that postbag because their own private letters were locked therein, and if Sir Timothy was out on the estate or engaged in his Justice Room, they had to wait until he was ready, or chose, to unlock it. They accused him of examining the handwriting and postmarks of their correspondence and of asking inquisitive questions about it. Which he may at some time have done, for, in Laura's time, they had betting tips and bookmakers' circulars addressed to the Post Office to be called for.

It was this matter of the postbag which had caused their animosity towards Laura. When she had first appeared as postwoman they had asked – or, rather, told – her to bring up to the house with the bag their letters addressed to the Post Office. Miss Lane, who was a stickler for strict observance of the official rules, would not permit her to do this. If a letter was addressed to the Post Office to be called for, she said, called for it must be, and although Laura, who thought it unfair that their letters should be inspected, like those of small boys at school, had softened Miss Lane's message to them when delivering it, they were annoyed and under a show of boisterous horseplay visited their annoyance upon Laura.

They would creep silently up behind her and clap her heavily upon the shoulders, or knock her hat over her eyes, or ruffle her hair with their hands, or try to kiss her. The maids, several of whom were often present, as the housekeeper and the butler were at that time taking their morning coffee in the housekeeper's room, would only laugh at her discomfiture, or join in the sport, putting pebbles down her neck, or flicking her face with their dusting-brushes.

'You look as if you'd been drawn through a quickset hedge backward,' remarked the head gardener's wife one day when Laura was more than usually dishevelled; but, when told what had happened, she only laughed and said: 'Well, you're only young once. You must get all the fun you can. You give them as good as they give you and they'll soon learn to respect you.' She dared not tell Miss Lane, for she knew that lady would complain to Sir Timothy and there would be what she thought of as 'a fuss'. She preferred to endure the teasing, which, after all, occupied but a few minutes during an outing in which there were rich compensations.

Excepting the men working in the fields, she seldom saw any one between the houses on her round. Now and then she would meet the estate carpenter with his bag of tools, going to mend a fence or a gate, and occasionally she saw Sir Timothy himself, spud in hand, taking what he called 'a toddle round the estate', and he would greet her in his jovial way as 'our little Postmistress-General' and tell her to go to Geering, the head gardener, and ask him to show her through the glasshouses and give her some flowers. Which was kind of him, but unnecessary, as Mr Geering had, on his own responsibility, conducted her several times through the long, warm, damp, scented hothouses, picking a flower here and there to add to her bouquet. *My* glasshouses, the gardener called them; *our* glasshouses, said his wife when speaking of them; to the actual owner they were merely *the* glasshouses. So much for the privilege of ownership!

Once she saw Sir Timothy in a more serious mood. That was after a night of high wind had brought down two magnificent elm trees on the edge of the ha-ha, and he called to her to come and look at the damage. It was a sad sight. The trees were lying with their roots upended and their trunks slanting across the ditch to the ruin of broken branches and smashed twigs on the lower level. Sir Timothy appeared to be as much distressed as if they had been the only trees he possessed. There were tears in his eyes as he kept repeating: 'Wouldn't have lost them for worlds! Known them all my life. Opened my eyes upon them, in fact, for I was born in that room there. See the window? It's this damned sunk fence is to blame. No root room on one side. Wouldn't have lost them for worlds!' And she left him lamenting.

Although so few people were seen there at the early hour of Laura's passing, the park was open to all. Couples went there for walks on summer Sundays, and the poorer villagers were permitted to pick up the dead fallen wood for their fires; but the copses and other enclosures were barred, especially in the spring, when the game birds were nesting. There were notice boards in such places to say trespassers would be prosecuted and, although Laura considered herself to some extent a privileged person, she climbed into them stealthily and kept a look-out for the gamekeeper. But he was an old man, getting beyond his work, people said; his cottage stood in a clearing in a wood on the other side of the estate, and she never once sighted him.

She went in and out of the copses, gathering bluebells or wild cherry blossom, or hunting for birds' nests, and never saw anyone, until one May morning of her second year on the round. She had gone into one of the copses where a few lilies-of-the-valley grew wild, found half a dozen or so, and was just climbing down the high bank which surrounded the copse when she came face to face with a stranger. He was a young man in rough country tweeds and carried a gun over his shoulder. She thought for a moment that he might be one of Sir Timothy's nephews, or some other visitor at the great house, though, of course, she should have remembered that no guest of Sir Timothy's would have carried a gun at that season. But, when he pointed to a notice board which said *Trespassers will be prosecuted* and asked, rather roughly, what the devil she thought she was doing there, she knew he must be a gamekeeper, and he turned out to be a new under-keeper engaged to do most of the actual work of the old man, who was failing in health, but refused to retire.

He was a tall, well-built young man, apparently in the middle twenties, with a small fair moustache and very pale blue eyes which, against his dark tanned complexion, looked paler. His features might have been called handsome but for their set rigidity. These softened slightly when Laura held out her half-dozen lilies-of-the-valley as an excuse for her trespass. He was sure she had meant to do no harm, he said, but the pheasants were still sitting and he could not have them disturbed. There had been too much of this trespassing lately – Laura wondered by whom – too much laxity, too much laxity, he repeated, as if he had just thought of the word and was pleased with it, but it had got to stop. Then, still walking close on her heels on the narrow path, as if to keep her in custody, he asked her if she would tell him the way to Foxhill Copse, as it was his first morning on the estate and he had not grasped the lie of the land yet. When she pointed it out and he saw that her own path led past, he unbent sufficiently to suggest that they should walk on together.

By the time they reached the copse he had become quite human. His name, he told her, was Philip White. His father was head gamekeeper on an estate near Oxford and he had so far worked under him, but had now come to Candleford Park on the understanding that when poor old Chitty died or retired he would take his place as head gamekeeper. Without actually saying so, he managed to convey the impression that by consenting to serve under Chitty for a time he was doing, not only Sir Timothy, but the whole neighbourhood a favour. His father's estate (he spoke of it as his father's in the way the Geerings spoke of 'our glasshouses') was larger and better preserved than this, and belonged to a very great nobleman with an historic title. He did not claim the title as a family possession, but it was evident that he felt its reflected glory.

Laura glanced up at him. No. He was perfectly serious. There was no smile on his face, not even a twinkle in his pale eyes; the only expression there was one of a faint interest in herself. Before they parted she had been shown a photograph of his sister, who worked in a draper's showroom in Oxford. It was that of a smiling girl in evening dress for some dance, with her fair hair dressed in curls high on her head. Laura was much impressed. 'All in our family are good-looking,' he said as he slipped the photograph back into his breast pocket. She had also been given a description of his parents' model cottage on the famous estate and been told of the owner's great shoots, to which dukes and lords and millionaires appeared to flock, and would probably have heard much more had not her conscience pricked her into saying: 'I really must go now, or I shall have to run all the way.' She had not told him anything about herself, nor had he asked any questions beyond inquiring where she lived and how often she passed that way. Happening to look back as she climbed over the stile, she saw him still standing where she had left him. He raised his hand in a wooden salute, and that, she thought, was the last she would see of him.

But she had not seen the last of Philip White. After that he always seemed to appear at some point on her walk. At first he would spring out of some copse with his gun and seem to be surprised to see her; but soon he would stroll openly along the path to meet her, then turn and walk by her side through the park until just before they came in sight of the great house windows. Beyond telling Miss Lane as an item of news on the first morning that a new under-keeper had come and that he had asked her the way to Fox'lls, Laura mentioned these meetings to no one, and as they met on the loneliest part of her round no one she knew ever saw them together. But for weeks they met almost daily and talked, or rather Philip talked and she listened. Sometimes he would take the hand which swung by her side and hold it in his as they walked on together. It was pleasant at sixteen to be the object of so much attention on the part of a grown man and from one who was spoken of respectfully by the villagers as Keeper White, while to her in secret he was Philip. 'Call me Philip,' he had said at their second meeting. 'I wouldn't allow any one else here to call me it, but I'd like it from you,' and she called him by that name occasionally. Never 'Phil'; it would not have suited him. He called her 'Laura', and once or twice when they passed through the kissing gate, he gave her a shy, cold, wooden kind of kiss over the bars.

She supposed they were sweethearts and sometimes looked into the future and saw herself feeding the pheasant chicks hatched out under hens in the little coops under the green clearing where old Chitty's cottage stood. She felt she could be happy for life in that pretty cottage on the green, surrounded by waving tree-tops. On one of her walks last spring she had seen the margins of the green and the earth under the trees starred with white wild anenomes, swaying in the wind, and it had looked to her then a perfect paradise. But then came the dampening thought that Philip would be there, too, at least some of the time, and she was not sure that she liked Philip well enough to be able to endure his perpetual company.

He was so self-satisfied, so sure that he and everything and everybody belonging to him were perfect, and he had no interests whatever outside his own affairs. If she tried to talk about other people or of flowers she had found, or some book she was reading, it was never long before he brought the conversation back to himself again. 'That's like *me*,' he would say, or, 'What *I* think about it is –' or, '*I* couldn't stand that sort of thing,' and she, who loved to listen to most people and found nearly everybody else interesting, wanted to run straight away across the park and fields and leave him talking to himself.

But she was constitutionally incapable of that. And if she tried to offend and quarrel with him, she could not. She knew that from some of the stories against himself he repeated, without the least idea that they were against himself. If she told him openly that she thought they ought not to walk together, as it was against official rules, she would still have to meet and pass him frequently, for it was one of his duties to patrol every part of the estate. There really seemed to be nothing she could do about it, except to bound on a few yards in front as they approached the kissing gate.

Then, when she least expected it, the whole affair came to a head and was over. It was just upon closing time one evening, and she had taken some forms to Miss Lane, who was already seated at the kitchen table about to begin on her accounts, when the office doorbell tinkled and she hurried back to find Philip there. That, to begin with, was a surprise to her, for he had never been in the office before – an embarrassment, too, for she knew that Miss Lane, sitting quietly at the kitchen table with the door wide open, would hear every word that was said. But there he was, looking full of impor-tance, and all she could do to cope with the situation was to say 'Good evening' in what she hoped was a businesslike voice. She almost prayed that he would say, 'Three penny stamps' or something of that kind and go. He might squeeze her hand, if he liked; she did not care if he kissed her, if only he kissed her quietly and Miss Lane did not hear. But she was not to be let off so easily.

Without any formal greeting, he pulled a letter out of his pocket and said: 'Can you get off for a few days at the end of this week? Well, as a matter of fact, you must. I've got this letter from our Cath' – his sister – 'and she says our Mum says I'm to bring you. Saturday to Monday, she says, or longer if we can manage it, but, of course, I can't. Nobody can afford to leave my job for long together – too many bad characters about. Still, I think I have earned a day or two and Sir Timothy's quite agreeable, so you'd better arrange about it now and I'll wait.'

Laura looked at the open door; she could positively feel Miss Lane listening. 'I'm s-s-sorry –' she began feebly, but the idea of any one trying to refuse an invitation from his family was unthinkable to Philip. 'Go and ask,' he commanded; then, more gently, but still too, too audibly: 'Go and ask. You've got the right. Everybody takes their girl for their people to see; and you are my girl, aren't you, Laura?'

The papers on the kitchen table rustled, then again dead silence, but Laura was no longer thinking of the danger of being overheard so much as wondering what she should say.

'You are my girl, aren't you, Laura?' asked Philip once more, and for the first time since she had known him, Laura detected a faint note of uneasiness in his voice. She herself was trembling with consternation, but when she said, 'You've never asked me,' her voice sounded flippant, perhaps coquettish, for Philip took one of her trembling hands and smiled down upon her as he said magnanimously: 'Well, I thought you understood. But don't be frightened. You will be my girl. Won't you, Laura?' That was inadequate enough as a declaration of love, but Laura's answer was even more inadequate: 'No – no thank you, Philip,' she said, and the most unromantic love scene on record was over, for, without another word, he turned, went out of the door and out of her life. She never saw him again to speak to. On one occasion, months afterwards, she had a momentary view of his distant figure, gun on shoulder, stalking across one of the open spaces of the park, but, if he ever came her way again, he must have chosen a time of day when she was not likely to be there.

But Miss Lane was still with her and had to be dealt with. Laura expected at least a severe scolding. A letter might even be written to her mother. But when Laura returned to the kitchen Miss Lane, who was carefully ruling a line in red ink, did not even look up. 'Who was that?' she asked in a casual tone when she had finished, and Laura, trying to sound casual too, replied: 'Sir Timothy's new gamekeeper.' No more was said at that moment, but, as she folded her accounts and slipped them into the large brown paper envelope with the printed address, 'Accountant-General, G.P.O., London', Miss Lane eyed Laura closely and said: 'You seem to know that young man very well.' 'Yes,' admitted Laura. 'I've met him on the round sometimes.' And Miss Lane said, 'Umph! So I gathered.'

So there were no reproaches. On the contrary, Miss Lane appeared in a better temper than usual for the rest of the evening. As they were lighting their candles to go up to bed, she said thoughtfully: 'I don't see why you should ever leave here. You and I get on very well together, and perhaps, after my time, you might take my place in the office.'

In after years Laura sometimes looked rather wistfully back on that evening when an apparent choice was offered her between two widely differing paths in life. It would have been pleasant to have lived all her days in comparative ease and security among the people she knew and understood. To have watched the seasons open and fade in the scenes she loved and belonged to by birth. But have we any of us a free choice of our path in life, or are we driven on by destiny or by the demon within us into a path already marked out? Who can tell?

Choice or no choice, Laura's sojourn at Candleford Green was to be but of a few years' duration. And, if the choice had been hers and she had remained there, her life might not have been as happy and peaceful as she afterwards imagined it would have been. Her mother's judgement was usually sound, and she had often told her: 'You're not cut out for a pleasant, easy life. You think too much!' Sometimes adding tolerantly: 'But we are as we are made, I suppose.'

X

Change in the Village

The gradual change which was turning the formerly quiet and secluded village of Candleford Green into the suburb of a small country town was accentuated by the death of Mr Coulsdon and the arrival of the new vicar. Mr Delafield was a young man in the early thirties, somewhat inclined to premature bulkiness, whose large, pink, clean-shaven face had a babyish look, which his fair hair, worn rather long and inclined to curl, did nothing to dispel. Dignity did not enter into his composition. He would run out to post a letter or to buy a cucumber for lunch in his shirt-sleeves, and, even when fully dressed, the only evidence of his sacred calling was his collar. Well-worn flannels and a Norfolk jacket were his usual everyday wear. Very dark grey, of course; any lighter shade would have been too revolutionary, as would anything more daring in the way of headgear than the black-and-white speckled straw boater he wore in summer in place of the round, black, soft felt hat of the other local clergy.

He looked like a very big boy, and an untidy boy. Miss Lane once said that she longed to take a needle and thread and set forward the top button of his trousers, so that he could button in the bulge at his waist. He probably thought Miss Lane's appearance as unsatisfactory as she did his, for he had come there with a townsman's ideas of the country, according to which a village postmistress should have worn a white apron and spoken the dialect. But he had come to his country living determined to be friendly with all his parishioners, and although Laura felt sure he did not like that sardonic little glint of amusement in her eyes when he tried to talk improvingly to her, he was always pleasantly breezy in his manner, and she, in time, came to admit that he had a boyish charm.

The verdict of others varied. The old order had changed and, in changing, had gone somewhat ahead of the times in the depth of the country. Some complained that his 'Hail fellow, well met!' attitude to everybody annoyed them. All men were brothers in church, of course, but outside they thought a clergyman ought to 'hold on to his dignity'. 'Look at poor old Mr Coulsdon! He was a gentleman, if ever there was one!' Others liked Mr Delafield because he was 'not proud and stuck up', like some parsons they could name. By the majority, judgement was suspended. 'You've got to summer and winter a man before you can pretend to know him' was an old country maxim much quoted at that time. On one point all churchgoers agreed; the new Vicar was a good preacher. He had a surprisingly deep, rich voice for one of his boyish appearance, and he used this to advantage in the pulpit.

Pride was certainly not one of Mr Delafield's failings. He had a charming way of relieving any old woman he met of any burden she was carrying. Once Laura saw him crossing the green with a faggot of sticks on his shoulder, and, on another occasion, he helped to carry home a clothes-basket of washing.

On leaving the Post Office, he would vault over the railings of the green to bowl for small boys playing cricket with an old tin for wicket. But that was in his early days; before he had been there long, Candleford Green cricket was put upon a proper footing, with an eleven of young men and practice nights for boys. On Saturday afternoons in summer he himself played with the eleven, and soon other local teams were challenged and the white flannels of such players as possessed them enlivened the pleasant, summery scene on the greensward.

Before long he had got together a club for boys which met in the schoolroom on winter evenings. The noise the boys made, said those who lived near, made life pretty well unbearable; but the boys' parents were pleased to have them kept out of mischief, and those who lived near their former winter evening haunts were not sorry. Then a timely Confirmation ceremony brought together the nucleus of a Girls' Guild which had its headquarters in the now disused servants' hall at the vicarage. Mrs Delafield was Lady President of this, but as she had two children and kept but one young maid in a house where there had formerly been four, she had little time for the supervision of the weekly meetings, and help had to be obtained from the ladies of the congregation. The Pratts, *Miss* Ruby and *Miss* Pearl, as the Vicar and his wife were careful to insist upon when naming them to the girls, saw and seized here their opportunity, and soon what they did not know about the vicarage household could easily, as people said, have been written on a threepenny bit.

The Delafields were poor. Soon after their arrival they gave out that, as the living was but a poor one and they had no private means, the charities of the former Vicar would have to be discontinued. 'I know myself what it is to be poor,' the Vicar would say frankly when sympathizing with one of the cottagers, and, although his hearer might smile incredulously as she mentally compared his idea of poverty with her own, his frankness would please her.

After a time, the tradesmen hinted that the new vicarage family was long-winded in paying its bills. 'But,' they would add, 'so far they've always paid up in the end, and they don't go running to another shop with their bit of ready money as soon as they owe you a few pounds, and they aren't extravagant,' which, from a shopkeeper's point of view, was not altogether a bad character to give a customer.

The Delafields had a succession of untrained young maids, of whom they expected trained service, and, in consequence, they were as often without a maid as with one. And they fared little better with the women brought in 'to oblige'. One excellent charwoman in her own line of washing and scrubbing was so taken aback on her first appearance at the vicarage by having a written list of the dishes she was expected to cook for dinner thrust into her hand that she seized her coarse apron and basket and bolted.

But what struck the Miss Pratts more than the scrappy meals and undusted rooms at the vicarage was what they called Mrs Delafield's 'singularity'. Her style of dress was what Miss Ruby called 'arty'. She wore long, loose frocks, usually terracotta or sage green, which trailed on the floor behind her and had low necks which exposed the throat when other women were whaleboned up to the ears.

For church on Sundays the Delafield children wore white kid slippers and openwork socks, but at all other times they ran about barefoot, which shocked the villagers and could not have been very comfortable for themselves, although they appeared to enjoy scrabbling with their toes in the dust or taking impressions of their own footprints in mud. Their ordinary everyday dress was a short brown holland smock, elaborately embroidered, which for comfort and beauty would have compared favourably with the more formal attire of other children of their class had it not invariably been grubby.

'Those awful children!' some people called them, but to others their intelligence and good looks made up for their lack of manners. And, 'Thank heaven,' somebody said, 'we ain't expected to "Miss" them!' It was something of a privilege to be able to say 'Elaine' or 'Olivia' when speaking to or of them, at a time when other quality children were 'Master' or 'Miss' in their cradles. The village had taken its lead in this matter from the Vicar, who always spoke to them of his children by their plain Christian names. Other parents added the prefix, often emphasizing it. One child Laura knew who, being the youngest of her family, retained the name and status of baby while a toddler, was spoken of by her parents to the servants and estate workers as 'Miss Baby'.

The change at the vicarage did as much as anything to hasten the decline of the old servile attitude of the poorer villagers. With all his failings, or what they considered failings, Mr Delafield did at least meet them on a purely human footing and speak to them as one man to another, not as one bending down from a pedestal. The country gentlemen around still loomed larger than life-size upon their horizon, but the Vicar lived amongst them, they saw him and spoke to him daily, and his example and influence were greater. Some still sighed for the fleshpots and blankets of the old régime, others regretted its passing from love of the stately old order, but a far larger number rejoiced, if insensibly, in the new democratic atmosphere of parochial life. The parish was soon to be proud of its Vicar.

From the first Mr Delafield's sermons had been praised by his congregation. 'Keeps you awake, he do', said some who had formerly been in the habit of nodding in sermon time. Their duty towards their neighbour and the importance of honesty and truthfulness had been topics too familiar to keep their eyes open, but when a sermon began: 'The other day I heard a man in this parish say –' or 'You may have read in your newspapers last week –' they sat up and listened.

Quite often the thing heard or read was amusing, and, although, of course, there could be no laughter in church, a slight stir of smiling appreciation would lighten the atmosphere and prepare the congregation to settle down happily to listen to the lesson or moral to be drawn. It was never a severe one. Hell was never mentioned, nor, for the matter of that, heaven, and earth was depicted as not as bad a place, after all, if people bore one another's burdens and pulled together. If, sometimes, the deep, melodious voice in the pulpit preached repentance, it was not so much repentance of the sins common in country villages as those of the world in general. No one present could ever feel hurt or offended by anything he said in his sermons. Indeed, a member of his congregation was heard to say in the churchyard one Sunday morning: 'A sermon like that makes you feel two inches taller.'

Those comfortable words, that eloquent voice, and the telling pauses when, leaning far over the edge of his pulpit, he searched the faces and seemed to look into the very hearts of his congregation, soon won for him the reputation of being the best preacher in the neighbourhood – some said in the country. People from surrounding parishes and even from Candleford town itself were soon coming to hear him preach. On summer Sunday evenings the church was often so well filled that latecomers had to stand in the aisle. Even Miss Lane, who was not a frequent churchgoer, attended a service. Back at home her only comment was: 'All very pleasant! But pass me my Darwin, please. Like the birds, I need a little grit in my food.'

But the lack of enthusiasm shown by one crusty old woman was but as a grain of sand on the seashore compared to the rising tide of the new Vicar's popularity as a preacher, which reached its high-water mark on Harvest Thanksgiving Sunday, when the *Candleford News* sent a reporter to take down the Vicar's sermon verbatim. Copies of the issue containing the sermon were bought in great numbers to be posted to sons and daughters in London, in the North of England, or out in the Colonies. 'Just to show them,' their parents said, 'that Candleford Green's no longer the poor little stick-in-the-mud spot they may be thinking.'

As Mr Delafield's popularity as a preacher increased and brought renown to the village, his small unconventionalities were accepted as the little, amusing, lovable peculiarities of genius. His wife had no longer difficulties with her maids and charwomen, for an elderly farmer's daughter proposed herself and was accepted as mother's help. By the time Laura left Candleford Green, the ladies of the congregation were almost fighting over decorating the church and the turns they had agreed to take at relieving Mrs Delafield of the family mending. So many pairs of carpet slippers were worked for Mr Delafield that only a centipede could have worn out all of them, and Elaine and Olivia were so frequently asked out to tea, and so feasted when there, that, had they not been sent away to a boarding school, their digestions would have been ruined. By his poorer parishioners, though not perhaps as respected as Mr Coulsdon had been, the new Vicar was more beloved, because more human.

Mr Delafield's cure of souls at Candleford Green was but brief. A year or two after Laura had left there she was told in a letter that he had accepted a London living and was to hold a special service in his new church for the Candleford Green Mothers' Meeting on its annual outing. But he left his mark on the village, not only by the spiritual comfort he had been able to bring to many, but also by breaking down prejudices.

Then, about that time, came a rise in wages. Agricultural workers were given fifteen instead of ten or twelve shillings a week, and skilled craftsmen were paid an agreed rate per hour, instead of the former weekly wage irrespective of the time put in, and although at the same time prices were rising, they had not as yet risen in proportion. The Boer War, when it came, sent prices soaring, but that was still several years in the future.

Meanwhile, Queen Victoria had her Diamond Jubilee and 'Peace and Plenty' was the country's watchword. Rural councils were established and some of the progressive Candleford Green villagers were able to voice their improvement schemes and to get a few of them carried out. There were rumours of scholarships for village schoolchildren; the County Council sent a cookery expert to lecture in the schoolroom; and there were evening classes, no longer called 'night school', for the older boys. Housing was still left to private enterprise, but the demand for more modern homes did not go unregarded.

When one of the Candleford Green villagers had a stroke of good luck in the way of a better job or higher wages, his wife's reaction to the good news would usually be to exclaim: 'Now we can go to live in one of the villas!' Sometimes her ambition was realized and they exchanged their old, inconvenient, though thick-walled and warm old cottage with its large, fertile garden for one of a row of small houses on the newly opened building estate on the Candleford Road.

The new house might prove to be damp and draughty, for the walls were thin and the woodwork ill-fitted, and the garden at the back of the house, formerly part of a damp, tussocky meadow, left in the rough by the builder, would certainly turn out what her husband would call 'a heartache'; but, as compensation, she would enjoy the distinction conferred by owning a smart front door with a brass knocker, a bay window in the parlour, and water laid on to the kitchen sink. Plus the *éclat* of living in one of the villas.

Although the speculative builder had left the making of the back garden to his tenant, he had finished the small plot in front by laying a few feet of turf round a small centre flower bed. Ornate iron railings enclosed this small space and a red-and-blue-tiled path led up to the front door. Outside, at the edge of the sidewalk, young trees had been planted, of which some had already died and others were pining, but, lining the favourite and most built-up road, a sufficient number survived to give colour to its name of Chestnut Avenue.

In Laura's time, a few of the villas were occupied by ambitious Candleford Green families which had migrated; more had been taken by clerks and shopmen from Candleford town who fancied a country life or wished to reduce their rent. Six shillings a week for a five-roomed villa was certainly not excessive, but no doubt it repaid the builder-owner well enough for his outlay. Laura's uncle, who was also a builder in Candleford, declared that the villas were run up of old oddments of second-hand stuff, without proper foundations, and that the first high wind would blow half of them down; but his pessimism may have been due to professional rivalry, though, to do him justice, it must be said that he spoke the truth when he frowned and shook his head and declared: 'Never touch a cheap job. Not my line.'

Chestnut Avenue stood, apparently firmly, as long as Laura lived near and may quite probably be standing now, let at treble the rent to trebly paid wage-earners, with the chestnut trees fully grown and candled with blossoms and a wireless mast in every back garden. As they were built, almost before the paint was dry the villas were occupied and the new tenants tied back their lace curtains with blue or pink ribbon and painted on the gate the name of their choice: 'Chatsworth' or 'Naples' or 'Sunnyside' or 'Herne Bay'.

Laura, although conscious of disloyalty to 'the trade', personified for her by her father and uncle, still thought the Chestnut Avenue houses stylish. She had just enough taste, or sense of humour, to think some of the names chosen for them by the occupiers were unsuitable – 'Balmoral' was the latest addition – but she saw nothing amiss with the wide-ribbon pale blue or pink curtain ties, though she herself would have preferred green or yellow. Except for the ex-villagers whom she already knew, the villas were occupied by a class of people which was new to her, the lower fringe of the lower middle class, of which she was to see a great deal later.

Her first introduction to this, to her, new way of life she owed to a Mrs Green of 'The Shack', the wife of a clerk in the Candleford Post Office. She had come to know the husband in the way of business, he had introduced her to his wife, and an invitation to tea had followed.

The Greens' villa was only distinguishable from the others by its name and by the maidenhair fern which stood in place of the usual aspidistra on a little table exactly in the centre of the small space between the draped curtains at the parlour window. Mrs Green said aspidistras were common, and Laura soon discovered that she had a great dislike of common things and especially of common people. The people who lived next door, she told Laura, were 'awfully common'. The man was a jobbing gardener, 'a clodhopper' she called him, and his wife wore his cloth cap when she hung out her washing. They were toasting herrings, morning, noon, and night, and the smell was 'most offensive'. She thought the landlord ought to be more particular in choosing his tenants. Laura, who was used to the ways of those she called 'clodhoppers' and their wives, and herself enjoyed a good bloater toasted on the coals for supper, heard this with wonder. Of course men who worked on the land were common, there were so many of them, but then there were a good many men in every other trade or calling, so why complain of the number? When it gradually dawned upon her that Mrs Green used the word 'common' in a social sense, she was rather afraid that she would be thought common, too; but she need not have feared, for that lady did not think of her at all, excepting as the possessor of eyes and ears.

Mrs Green was a small, fair woman, still under thirty, who would have been pretty had not her face habitually worn a worried expression which sharpened her features and was already destroying her bloom. Her refinement, or perhaps her means, did not run to visits to a dentist and, to hide decaying teeth, she cultivated a thin, close-lipped little smile. But her hair was still very pretty and beautifully cared for, and she had pretty hands which she rubbed with cold cream after washing the tea things.

Her husband was also small and fair, but his manners were more simple and his expression was opener and franker than that of his wife. When he laughed, he laughed loudly, and then his wife would look at him reproachfully and say in a pained voice, '*Albert!*' He had not had the same training in the art of keeping up appearances as his wife, for while she, as she said, had come down in the world, having been born into what she vaguely termed 'a refined family', he had begun to earn his living as a telegraph messenger and worked his way up to his present position, which, though still modest, was in those days something of an achievement. Left to himself, he would have been a pleasant, homely kind of fellow who would have enjoyed working in his garden and afterwards sitting down in his shirt-sleeves to a bloater or tinned salmon for tea. But he had married a genteel wife and she had educated him as far as possible up to her own standard.

They were both touchingly proud of their home, and Laura on her first visit had to be shown every nook and corner of it, including the inside of the cupboards. It was furnished in accord with its architectural style. The parlour, which they called the 'drawing-room', had a complete suite of furniture upholstered in green tapestry, and there was a green carpet, but not quite the right shade of green, on the floor. Photographs in ornate frames stood on little tables and a set of framed pictures on the walls illustrated the courtship of an insipid looking couple – 'Lovers' Meeting', 'The Letter', 'Lovers' Quarrel', and 'Wedded'. There was not a book or a flower in the room and not so much as a cushion awry to show that it was lived in. As a matter of fact, it was not. It was more a museum or a temple or a furniture showroom than a living-room. They sat in state in the bay window on Sunday evenings and watched their neighbours pass by, but took their meals and spent the rest of their time in the kitchen, which was a much pleasanter room.

In the bedroom above the parlour there was one of the new duchess dressing-tables and a wardrobe with a long looking-glass door. These pieces of furniture Mrs Green pointed out as 'the latest', a description she also applied to many other treasured objects which she seemed to regard as models of fashion and elegance. Knowing only the cottage simplicity of her own home and the substantial but old-fashioned comfort of Miss Lane's and her Candleford relatives' houses, Laura had to accept her word for this. The people whom she had hitherto known just put what they had or could get into their homes, old things and new things, side by side with each other, with, perhaps, a few yards of new chintz or a new coat of paint to smarten things up occasionally. So, naturally, they did not make a show of their houses, beyond sometimes pointing out some special treasure which had 'belonged to my old granny' or 'been in our family for years and years'.

There were no such out-of-date objects in the Greens' home; everything there had been bought by themselves when setting up house or later, and the date of purchase and even the price were subjects for conversation. Seven pounds for the drawing-room suite and ten pounds for that in the bedroom! Laura was amazed; but then, she reflected, the Greens were comfortably off; Mr Green's weekly salary must be at least two pounds.

Everything was beautifully kept, furniture and floors were highly polished, windows gleamed, curtains and counterpanes were immaculate, and the little kitchen at the back of the house was a model of neatness. Laura found out afterwards that Mrs Green worked herself nearly to death. With only one child and a house only a little larger than theirs, she worked twice the number of hours and spent ten times the energy of the cottage women. They, standing at their doors with their arms folded, enjoying a gossip with a neighbour, would often complain that a woman's work was never done; but the Mrs Greens were working away while they gossiped and, afterwards, when they were indoors having 'a set down with a cup o' tay', the Mrs Greens, wearing gloves, were polishing the silver. For, of course, forks and spoons and any other metal objects possessed by a Green housewife were known collectively as 'the silver', even if there was not one single hallmark to be seen upon any of them.

At the tea-table it was the turn of the Greens' only child to be chief exhibit. Doreen was seven and, according to her parents, there never had been and never again would be such an intelligent child. 'So cute. You should hear some of her sayings,' and specimens were repeated forthwith, the little girl meanwhile munching her cake with a self-conscious expression. She was a pretty, well-mannered child, well dressed and well cared for, and not so much spoiled as might have been expected. Her parents adored her, and it came as a shock to Laura to hear one of them say and the other repeat that they did not intend to have any more children. Not *intend* to have more! What say would they have in the matter? If married people had one child, they almost always had more – a good many more in most cases. Laura had sometimes heard the mother of a seventh or eighth say that she hoped it would be the last, 'Please God', but she had never before heard one say definitely that it would be. Miss Lane, when told of this incident, said she didn't think much of the Greens for talking like that before a girl of Laura's age; but, as a matter of fact, people nowadays had learned how to limit their families, and a good thing, too, she thought. 'But you don't want to trouble your head about anything to do with marriage,' she concluded, 'and if you take my advice you won't ever do so. Leave marriage to those who are suited for it.' But Laura thought she would like some children, a girl and two boys, perhaps, and to have a house of her own with lots of books in it and no suites of furniture at all, but all sorts of odd, interesting things, such as Miss Lane had.

Her acquaintance with the Greens brought Laura for the first time in contact with the kind of people among whom much of her life was to be spent. It was a class newly emerging in this country, on the borderline between the working and middle classes. Its main type had many good points. Those belonging to it were industrious, frugal and home-loving. Their houses were well kept, their incomes well managed, and their ambitions on their children's behalf knew no bounds. No sacrifice on the part of the parents was too great if, by it, they could give a better start in life than their own to their offspring. The average number of children in a family was two, but there were many only children and nearly as many childless homes; a family of three was unusual.

The men's suits were kept well brushed, sponged and pressed by their wives, and the women had the knack of dressing well on little. Many of them were able to make, alter, and bring up to date their own clothes. They were good cooks and managers; their homes, though often tasteless, were substantially furnished and beautifully kept; and, although when alone they might take their meals in the kitchen, they had elaborate afternoon tea-cloths and fashionable knick-knacks for the table for festive occasions.

Those were the lines along which they were developing. Spiritually, they had lost ground, rather than gained it. Their working-class forefathers had had religious or political ideals; their talk had not lost the raciness of the soil and was seasoned with native wit which, if sometimes crude, was authentic. Few of this section of their sons and daughters were churchgoers, or gave much thought to religious matters. When the subject of religion was mentioned, they professed to subscribe to its dogmas and to be shocked at the questioning of the most outworn of these; but, in reality, their creed was that of keeping up appearances. The reading they did was mass reading. Before they would open a book, they had to be told it was one that everybody was reading. The works of Marie Corelli and Nat Gould were immensely popular with them. They had not sufficient sense of humour to originate it, but borrowed it from music-hall turns and comic papers, and the voice in which such gems were repeated was flat and toneless compared to the old country speech.

But those who had left village life and all it stood for behind them were few compared to the number of those who stayed at home and waited for change to come to them. Change came slowly, if surely, and right into the early years of this century many of the old village ways of living remained and those who cherished the old customs were much as country people had been for generations. A little better educated, a little more democratic, a little more prosperous than their parents had been, but still the same unpretentious, warm-hearted people, with just enough malice to give point to their wit and a growing sense of injustice which was making them begin to inquire when their turn would come to enjoy a fair share of the fruits of the earth they tilled.

They, too, or, rather, their children and grandchildren, were to come in time to the parting of the ways when the choice would have to be made between either merging themselves in the mass standardization of a new civilization or adapting the best of the new to their own needs while still retaining those qualities and customs which have given country life its distinctive character. That choice may not even now have been determined.

But only a few of the wisest foresaw that the need for such a choice would arise when, for Laura, what appeared to be an opportunity offered and, driven on by well-meant advice from without and from within by the restless longing of youth to see and experience the whole of life, she disappeared from the country scene. To return often, but never as herself part of it, for she could only be that in her native county, where she had sprung from the soil.

On the last morning of her postwoman's round, when she came to the path between trees where she had seen the birds' footprints on the snow, she turned and looked back upon the familiar landmarks. It was a morning of ground mist, yellow sunshine, and high rifts of blue, white-cloud-dappled sky. The leaves were still thick on the trees, but dew-spangled gossamer threads hung on the bushes and the shrill little cries of unrest of the swallows skimming the green open spaces of the park told of autumn and change.

There was the stable tower with its clock-face and, near it, though unseen, was the courtyard where she had been annoyed – foolishly annoyed, she thought now – by the horseplay of the footmen. The chief offenders had gone long before and with those who had taken their places she knew quite well how to deal, even if they had been offensive, which they were not, for she was nearly three years older. There, where the path wound past the two copses, she had met Philip White – he, too, had left the estate – and away to the left were the meadows where the cows had obstructed her path. Farther on, quite out of sight, was the Post Office where, doubtless, Miss Lane was at that moment dispensing stamps with the air of a high priestess, still a little offended by what she considered Laura's desertion, but not too much so to have promised her as a parting gift one of her own watches and chains. And around the Post Office and green was the village where she had had good times and times not so good and had come to know every one of its inhabitants and to count most of them as her friends.

Nearer at hand were the trees and bushes and wild-flower patches beside the path she had trodden daily. The pond where the yellow brandyball waterlilies grew, the little birch thicket where the long-tailed tits had congregated, the boathouse where she had sheltered from the thunderstorm and seen the rain plash like leaden bullets into the leaden water, and the hillock beyond from which she had seen the perfect rainbow. She was never to see any of these again, but she was to carry a mental picture of them, to be recalled at will, through the changing scenes of a lifetime.

As she went on her way, gossamer threads, spun from bush to bush, barricaded her pathway, and as she broke through one after another of these fairy barricades she thought, 'They're trying to bind and keep me.' But the threads which were to bind her to her native county were more enduring than gossamer. They were spun of love and kinship and cherished memories.